TARANTULA SHOES

TARANTULA SHOES

Tom Birdseye

Holiday House/New York

Library of Congress Cataloging-in-Publication Data
Birdseye, Tom.
Tarantula shoes / Tom Birdseye. — 1st ed.
p.   cm.
Summary: After moving from Arizona to Kentucky with his parents,
his five-year-old twin brother and sister, and his pet tarantula,
Fang, an eleven-year-old works creatively to earn the money for a
special pair of basketball shoes that will help him feel accepted.
ISBN 0-8234-1179-6
[1. Moving, Household—Fiction.   2. Brothers and sisters—Fiction.
3. Twins—Fiction.   4. Tarantulas—Fiction.   5. Shoes—Fiction.]
I. Title.
PZ7.B5213Tar   1995   94-38424   CIP   AC

For the people of Kentucky—the Bluegrass State—
where basketball is king and conversation an art.

And for the Arizona desert rats I've come to know:
cactus fans, tarantula lovers.

Acknowledgments

Although writing is mostly a solitary task, turning a story into a book is not.

I especially want to acknowledge the expert guidance I have received on *Tarantula Shoes* (and on many other projects) from my editor, Margery Cuyler. Working behind the scenes, she rarely gets all the credit she deserves.

Also, thanks to John and Kate Briggs, and all the good people at Holiday House, for their warmth and support of me as a writer.

TOM BIRDSEYE
Corvallis, Oregon, 1994

Contents

TARANTULA SHOES

CHAPTER 1

511 Sycamore Street

"**W**elcome to Macinburg, Kentucky!" Dad said as he climbed out of the big U-Haul moving van.

I opened the door of the family station wagon but stayed seated.

Dad smiled at me. "Isn't it beautiful here, Ryan?"

I looked all around and tried to smile back at him. But right then lightning flashed and—KA-BLAMMO—a big clap of thunder boomed out of the clouds.

The twins, Justin and Ellie, ran over to where Mom stood on the sidewalk, looking up at our new house at 511 Sycamore Street. They grabbed hold of her legs and hid their faces. She reached down and stroked their red curls. "It's all right," she said. "It's only thunder."

Mom. She's always easy on those curtain climbers. I don't know how she does it. Only a minute earlier I'd been so sick of them singing "On Top of Spaghetti," I almost threw up. They must have sung it two hundred times!

"Yeah, it's only thunder," I said, more to myself than to the twins. I got out of the car and puffed out my chest, trying to act like someone who's almost twelve should act—brave and grown-up.

But deep down inside, I wasn't feeling very brave or grown-up. Not because of the thunder. I'd heard plenty of boomers during summer storms back in Arizona. I like them, the way the sound comes on with a sudden crack, then rolls around like it's chuckling because it made the little kids jump.

No, it wasn't the thunder. It was the upside-down way my life was feeling right then that had me scared. I'd been happy in my little town of Sierra, Arizona. I was born there and had lived in the same neighborhood all my life. I had friends I'd known since I was in preschool and one best friend ever: Patrick. He knew me as well as anybody. The Desert Rats, we called ourselves, when we went exploring up the canyon. But now Dad and Mom had done this awful thing—moved the whole family all the way across the country to this little town called Macinburg, Kentucky—and it had me as jittery as a chicken at the coyote café.

I looked around. Not a saguaro or ocotillo cactus in sight. No mesquite trees or palo verde. No whiptail lizards soaking in the sun. No gila woodpeckers. No rocks. Kentucky was covered up. The trees spread their limbs over the sidewalks like big green umbrellas. You could barely see the sky, which was all clouds anyway. And there was no dirt, just grass, mowed like it was supposed to be carpet. Bushes were everywhere. I was surrounded! Surrounded by green.

But the weirdest part was the air. It made my skin slick with sweat. My T-shirt was so wet it stuck to my back. I could hardly breathe! How could anybody want to live in a place where the air was too thick to get into your lungs? This place was downright scary.

I didn't let on, though. When you're the shortest kid your age—even shorter than the girls—you make a point to act big. "Yeah, it's just thunder," I said again. "Nothing to worry about."

Like it was trying to make a liar out of me, another flash of lightning and a big KA-BLAMMO went off nearby. I jumped, and Justin and Ellie let out nervous giggles.

But before I could get off a good warning glare in their direction, Dad said, "That was pretty close. I guess we'd better get inside before it starts to—"

ZZZZZACK! A jagged, crackling bolt of lightning tore across the sky directly over us, and the rain came down like it was dumped out of a bucket on top of our heads.

Mom and Dad and the twins ran for the front porch. I started to run after them but then remembered Fang, my pet tarantula. He was still on the backseat of the station wagon in his little glass terrarium. No way was I going to leave my best souvenir of the Arizona desert out there alone in the rain. Or my official NBA basketball. I jerked the car door open, grabbed them both, and ran after my family, big drops of rain pelting my back. Then I walked into my new home for the very first time.

New? Did I say *new?*

"This place was built in 1919!" Dad said proudly, standing in the middle of the empty living room.

Mom and Justin and Ellie all smiled up at him like they agreed.

I looked at the cracked plaster, chipped paint, dented woodwork, scuffed-up floor. Talk about ugly!

Dad glanced my way as if he could read my thoughts. "They knew how to build houses back then. Real craftsmanship," he said. "Sure it needs a little work . . ."

"A *little?*" I said under my breath.

Dad strode over to me, grinning like he'd won the lottery instead of bought a disaster with a roof on top. "But who can do a better job of fixing this place up than your mother and me?"

Mom walked our way, smiling. "Just give it a few days, Ryan," she said. "Once our things are unpacked and in place, you'll start to feel at home."

Dad leaned very close and his voice changed, dropping almost to a whisper. "This move is a great opportunity, Ryan."

Here it came again, what I'd heard too many times before. We had moved to Kentucky because an old high school friend had offered Dad a chance to be a partner in his construction business. Work was hard to get in Arizona, but there was plenty here in his old hometown.

For Mom, too. She had gotten a better job at the Bank of Macinburg than she'd had at Sierra Trust in Arizona. "Instead of a teller, I'll be a financial service representative!"

I didn't know what a financial service representative was, but from the tone of her voice and Dad's big grin, I figured that for them it all boiled down to "a great opportunity." To top it all off, we'd be a lot closer to relatives, they kept saying. Grandma O'Keefe lived just a couple of hours away, in Ohio. And Oma and Opa were only a little farther in the other direction, in some place called Corbin, where

Mom had grown up. We'd even get to visit with our cousins down in Atlanta on holidays!

Mom would talk of it all and smile. Dad would nod and say, "A great opportunity." Over and over and over he'd say it.

But right then I didn't feel like listening again, so I told them what they wanted to hear, even if I didn't mean it. (Sometimes you have to do that with adults—just say what they need you to say—so they'll get out of your face.) "I know," I said. "You guys loved it in Kentucky when you were kids."

The big grin crept back onto Dad's face. "And you will, too! *Especially* this house, once we get it fixed up." He winked. "There's a basketball hoop out back."

Mom put her arm around me. "And here you'll have your own room. No more sharing with Justin and Ellie."

I glanced over at the twins, who were trying to touch their tongues to their noses. The idea of having my own bedroom did sound good. They were always into my stuff in Arizona.

"Come see it!" Dad said. "It's got the same nice woodwork as the rest of the house and a big window with a view of the backyard. And it's private, too, off in its own corner."

I set Fang's terrarium down on the living room floor and leaned close to see if he was okay. I watched him crawl across the sand and move under the rock I had propped up for him. Just like me, I thought. He's homesick for the desert, for Arizona.

"Come on, Ryan," Mom said. "You'll love it!"

I set my official NBA basketball next to the terrarium, then followed Mom and Dad and the twins down a short hallway. Dad opened a door. "Ta-da!" he said, and flipped on the lights.

It was my very own bedroom . . . painted pink.

CHAPTER 2

Where Y'all From?

I let out a groan as Justin and Ellie danced around singing, "Ryan has a pink room! Ryan has a pink room!"

Dad looked over the walls. "Oh, well, yeah," he said, glancing at me. "I guess another color would be better, huh?"

I just stood and stared with my mouth hanging open. How could anyone have ever thought this was a good color to paint a room? The pink was so bright, it made my eyeballs vibrate.

"We'll put paint at the top of the shopping list," Mom said.

Dad grinned. "You bet! Just name the color,

Ryan. One . . . er, two coats and presto, a whole new feeling!"

I couldn't imagine even twenty coats doing the job.

"Is our room pink, too?" Ellie wanted to know. "I *love* pink."

"Or orange?" Justin asked. "Orange would be great!"

"I'll bet it's orange *and* pink!" Ellie offered.

Justin wiggled with excitement. "Yeah!"

"Can we see it? Can we see it?" they both sang.

"Sure, let's take a look," Dad said. He and Mom went upstairs with the twins, leaving me surrounded by all that pink. I closed my eyes and wished as hard as anyone has ever wished to be back where I belonged—Arizona.

Thunder rumbled not too far off, and rain plinked against my bedroom window glass. But through all that I heard another sound. Knock, knock, knock. It reminded me of *The Wizard of Oz*, when Dorothy clicked her heels together three times and wished to go home. I thumped the heels of my old basketball shoes together. There's no place like Arizona. There's no place like Arizona. There's no place like Arizona.

Knock, knock, knock.

I opened my eyes very slowly to see . . . pink.

Knock, knock, knock.

The door. The knocking sound was at our front door. I walked from my bedroom into the hall. "Mom?" I called up the stairs, hoping she'd go answer. "Dad?"

But they were still showing the twins their room. The knocking became very loud: KNOCK, KNOCK, KNOCK. I stepped back into the living room. A boy was peering in through the front screen door. He lowered his knocking hand as soon as he saw me. "Hi," he said. "Where y'all from?"

I took a few steps closer. "What did you say?"

The boy opened the screen door and stepped inside, letting a small brown dog in after him. Both had wiry hair and were wet from the rain. The boy, who looked about my age, was grinning, more out of one side of his mouth than the other, which made his eyebrows go lopsided. He spoke again. "I said, 'Where y'all from?' "

His words sounded like they were covered with maple syrup, kind of gooey with sliding sounds all over them. Mom had told me people would talk differently in Kentucky, with a southern accent, like she and Dad used to years ago, but still . . . It took a few seconds for the boy's words to sink in. He wanted to know where I'd moved from.

"Arizona," I answered.

"*Arizona?*" the boy said as if it were another planet. "I've lived across the street in that brick house yonder all my life." He stuck out his hand. "My name is Gordon, Gordon Schur."

No kids I had ever met shook hands unless their parents made them. But Gordon Schur acted like this was what everyone in Kentucky did, so I shook his hand, even though it felt weird.

"Howdy-do," Gordon said, shaking and shaking. His dog danced all around, its toenails clicking on the wooden floor, then shook its whole body, like it was saying howdy-do, too. Water went flying everywhere. I noted that a little of it got on Fang's terrarium. Being a desert critter, Fang doesn't like water, and I thought about moving him to a safer place.

But Gordon Schur still had hold of my hand and laughed—"Haw"—at his dog. Finally he let go of me and pointed at the mutt. "This is Colonel. We used to call him Alfred, but then he jumped up on the dining room table and swiped some fried chicken. We had to chase him all over the house to get it back. Dad said that was *real* fast food. Haw! Get it? Him running so fast with food in his mouth. So we decided to change Alfred to Colonel, after Colonel Sanders and his fast food Kentucky Fried Chicken. Haw! I laugh every time I think about it. Pretty funny, huh? Do you get it?"

"Uh, not really," I said, backing up a few steps and looking over my shoulder for Mom or Dad. Although I was beginning to understand more and more of the words the boy was saying—I guess my ears were getting kind of tuned in, like an antenna —I wasn't so sure I wanted to. Weird. This kid was weird.

Gordon grinned, and his eyebrows went lopsided again. "I'm going to be rich when I grow up, but this year I'll be twelve. How about you?"

"Twelve, too," I managed to get out.

"Great! Same grade! We can ride the bus together. Gotta go across town to get to junior high, you know. Yep, gonna get on the big yellow taxi with all those big kids and—"

"Wait a minute," I said, holding up my hand like a traffic cop. I stepped back toward Gordon Schur. I could have sworn he said he was going to be twelve soon, just like me, but that we'd be going to junior high. That was impossible. As well as I could remember, I had just finished fifth grade, and next was sixth. Sixth-graders don't go to junior high. That's later, in seventh grade. I must have heard wrong. This southern accent stuff was going to be tough. "You didn't say we'd go to junior high, did you?" I asked, leaning forward.

Gordon laughed. "Haw! I guess you hear as well

as you talk, being from Arizona and all. Sure, junior high. Some folks call it middle school, but here in Macinburg we still call it junior high, even though sixth-graders go, too. Dad says some things never change, like my Aunt Tilly. She won't quit eating chocolate, even though it makes her silly! Haw! Get it? Silly Tilly. Yep, junior high for you and I."

I felt myself turning to jelly in the knees. This couldn't be. I'd spent the whole summer imagining myself a sixth-grader at *elementary* school. Like a good movie that you want to watch again and again, I'd pictured it all in living color: Me walking down the hall, little first-graders stepping out of the way. Me sitting in the back row during assemblies, looking so cool. Me getting to raise the flag or make announcements over the school intercom—stuff sixth-graders get to do. And at the top of the list was me finally getting my turn to be a team captain for basketball during recess. No more older kids around to always be in charge. I'd have a chance to pick my team and prove I can dribble, pass, and shoot. Then people would see how great I really am, despite being short. They'd see that I'm going to make it to the pros some day: Ryan O'Keefe, NBA All-Star! Me, sixth-grader, cool guy, great basketball player. That's how I'd imagined all summer it would be, *even* in Kentucky.

"Tell me it's not junior high," I said. But just then lightning flashed outside again and a big clap of thunder shook the house.

Colonel let out a soft whine. Gordon reached down and petted him. Colonel snuffled at Gordon's hand and thumped his tail against Gordon's leg.

"Yep, junior high," Gordon said. "We'll be sixers."

"Sixers?" I said. The sound of the word made me feel queasy.

Gordon nodded. "Some things never change. We'll get picked on by the eighth-graders—and probably the seventh-graders, too. They'll call us sixers and jam our lockers by pounding pennies into the crack. Then we won't be able to get our books, and we'll end up being late for class and get sent to the principal, who I hear is as mean as ashcakes for Christmas. They'll block our way in the hall, too, and stuff us in trash cans and give us swirlies."

Swirlies? I was afraid to ask.

"They like messing with the little guys," Gordon went on. "We'll be the little guys, ya know."

Cold sweat began to form on my forehead. Being the size I am doesn't make the words *little guys* particular favorites. This was my worst nightmare, a real-life horror movie. What was next? Pimples? Hair in my nostrils?

"You have to switch classes all the time, too," Gordon continued, "which can get a person lost.

And they make you change into gym clothes for PE in front of *everybody!*"

This was all happening so fast. It was too confusing, too crazy to be real. My head was swimming, my stomach starting to roll.

Colonel, I noticed, was beginning to nose around Fang's terrarium. I leaned down and grabbed it off the living room floor. I was feeling downright sick and had trouble standing back up. Dad had it all wrong. Kentucky wasn't an opportunity, it was a *big* mistake. I looked down at Fang, now out from under his rock. *Don't worry, Fang, I'll do everything I can to get us home.*

"And then when you get on the bus," Gordon was saying, "the older kids take your stuff and—" He stopped short and pointed. "Hey, is that big hairy thing a *spider?*"

I looked down at Fang, my poor homesick Fang. "It's just a tarantula," I managed to get out.

Gordon grabbed Colonel by the collar and took a big step back. "Uh, I've got to get on home," he said, not taking his eyes off Fang. "Let's go for a bike ride tomorrow, maybe without the spider, huh? I'll show you Macinburg. Y'all are going to love it here!"

I watched numbly as Gordon beat a quick retreat out the front door. "Mom?" I called out, turning for help. "Dad?"

My stomach was doing dipsy-doodles and back

flips. Couldn't they open a few windows and let in some fresh air?

I staggered toward the hall. Where were my parents when I really needed them?

It turned out they were still upstairs trying to convince the twins to get out of a little closet in the hallway. I dragged myself to the second floor by the banister. Collapsing on the top stair, I explained about junior high, sure that if my parents heard what life for their eldest son was really going to be like in Kentucky, they'd be ready to head back west.

But Mom just said, "How wonderful! Junior high!"

My stomach did a double flip with a half twist as Dad added, "Sure! You'll do great with the big kids!"

Just then there was another flash of lightning—a gigantic bolt this time. The whole world lit up, and I could hear the crackling sound of electricity in the air. KA-BLAMMO! The house shook. The lights blinked twice, then went out.

It was very quiet for a second—a second in which the twins popped wide-eyed out of the little closet. Mom silently mouthed the words "Oh my," and I had a sudden, awful surge in my stomach.

But before I could rush through the nearest door,

hoping it was the upstairs bathroom, Dad burst into a big laugh and said, "Hey, just like in a horror movie!" He reached over and slapped me on the back like he'd told a really good one.

I threw up on his shoe.

CHAPTER 3

This Had Better Be Good

The next morning I woke up with Justin and Ellie staring me in the face. They held up their favorite stuffed animals so I could see. "Sleepy Bear and Hippo want Sugar Krinkles for breakfast," Ellie said.

I looked out the window of my pink bedroom. It was barely light outside. "It's too early to be up," I moaned. "I'm tired."

No wonder. Talk about a lousy night's sleep. Although the house had central air-conditioning, it didn't work. Dad had opened the windows after I barfed all over his shoe, but the hot, sticky air that came in from outside was no relief. I'd lain awake on sweat-soaked sheets, worrying about Kentucky and getting picked on at junior high school. "Leave me alone," I said to the twins. "Go back to bed."

Justin pushed his stuffed animal closer to my face. "But Hippo is hungry."

I covered my head with my pillow. "Go away!"

They didn't. Ellie yelled into the pillow, "Sleepy Bear and Hippo have got to eat now so they can help us get ready for the spaceman!"

The spaceman? I lifted my pillow far enough to see if the twins were grinning at their stupid early-morning joke.

They weren't.

"Yup," Justin said. "We found an old radio in that little closet upstairs. It came on all by itself this morning, and a spaceman started saying, 'Calling Planet Earth! Calling Planet Earth!' He's coming to visit us, Ryan, and we've got to get ready."

I started to say, "You guys are dumber than a fence post," but I didn't. Sometimes I amaze myself and am polite, even when I don't have to be. Besides, I knew from experience that insulting the twins wouldn't get them out of my life so I could get back to sleep. Maybe if I used a little logic, though. . . .

"Radios don't come on by themselves," I explained. "Spacemen don't call up and say they are dropping by for a visit, either."

These simple facts didn't seem to matter to Justin

and Ellie, though. They were always imagining un-
real stuff. When they were three, they spent a whole
month claiming that toe fairies were living in their
shoes, tickling them, making them laugh.

"The spaceman in the radio told us his name is
Quando," Justin said. "He's from some planet
called . . ."

"Neltoid," Ellie offered.

Justin nodded. "Yeah, Nel . . . Neltoid, and he's
coming to see us. He said to pat our heads and rub
our bellies at the same time if we could hear his
message."

Justin and Ellie patted their heads and rubbed
their bellies.

"Quando is coming to see us soon," Ellie said.
"We've got to get ready."

"But first we need to feed Sleepy Bear and Hippo
breakfast," Justin reminded me. "Sugar Krinkles,
not that healthy grain stuff."

I moaned, louder this time, and pulled my pillow
over my head. Ellie lifted it back up. "*Please*, Ryan.
Mom and Dad are still asleep."

Justin laughed. "Honk shoe! Honk shoe! That's
what Dad says when he sleeps."

I let out a big sigh. "Dad's snoring, so you pick on
me."

They both smiled and gave me a hug. "You're our
brother!"

"Don't remind me," I growled as I staggered out of bed.

The kitchen looked like the rest of the house—piles of boxes everywhere. Mom and Dad had dumped stuff all over the place so they could get the U-Haul truck in on time and not be charged an extra day of rental.

It took me a while, but I finally found a box of Sugar Krinkles. No milk, though. No bowls. No silverware. No table to eat at, either.

The twins sat down on the kitchen floor and ate Sugar Krinkles right out of the box, chattering on and on about the radio, the spaceman coming to visit, and how maybe when they started kindergarten they could take Quando in for show and tell.

"How do you know you'll even like kindergarten?" I asked.

Justin looked at me as if I had no sense and said, "Because."

I shook my head. Stupid little kids. They'd find out soon enough how hard life in Kentucky would be. "Think what you want," I said, "but promise to be quiet while you're doing it, and don't wake me up this early again for the rest of your lives, okay?"

They both nodded, and Ellie said, "Sleepy Bear and Hippo promise, too."

"Good," I said, and headed back toward my bedroom.

But it was too late. As I crossed the living room, the front door swung open and there was Gordon. "Well, look-a-here!" he said with his big grin and lopsided eyebrows. "The dead have done come to life!"

I tried to act like I didn't hear him, but he came on in anyway—his dog, too.

"I was going to let Colonel here wake you up," Gordon said. "You know, howl outside your window. I'll bet I could rent him as an alarm clock. I'd get rich quick! Haw!" He patted Colonel on the head. "You want to ride bikes downtown? We said we'd go if you leave that spider of yours here, remember?" He looked around the room. "You don't let that thing out, do you?"

"I don't feel like going for a bike ride," I said, continuing on toward my bedroom. If Gordon could walk into my house and start blabbing away without even so much as saying "Good morning," then I could forget the polite stuff, too.

Gordon didn't seem to notice my attitude, though. "You've *got* to see Ernie's Eatery, Ryan," he said cheerfully. "It's a new fast-food restaurant downtown. Fast food is the business of the future, you know. I used to think I'd be an undertaker when I grew up—my Uncle Warren is one and he's rich—but now I've changed my mind. Undertaking is a dying business, if you know what I mean. Get it? A *dying* business. Haw!"

I turned back and looked at Gordon. "You wanted to be an *undertaker?*" Just how weird can a person get?

Gordon nodded. "But I like fast food better now. That's where the money is—fast food. Even Colonel here knows that."

Gordon reached down to pat Colonel on the head just as Justin and Ellie appeared from the kitchen, still eating dry Sugar Krinkles out of the box. "Hi," Ellie said. "A spaceman is coming to visit us. His name is Quando. We've got to get ready."

Gordon shook his head as the twins ran past me and up the stairs toward their room. "Two of them, huh?" he said. "Man, I feel sorry for you. I've got one brother, J.T., and he drives me nuts. He never stops moving, even when he eats, like those two of yours! He runs laps around the table, and Mom pokes food in his mouth as he goes by. Never stops! My parents think he's cute as a button, though. I think he's just trouble." He grinned. "But there you are with two. Oooeee! Double trouble. I'll bet your parents think they're cute, too, huh?"

It was the first time Gordon had said anything that I agreed with. I nodded. "Yeah. One time the twins stuck their heads in the toilet and flushed it so they could feel that red curly hair going round and round in the water. I thought it was gross, but Mom and Dad laughed."

Gordon frowned. "Nothing funny about a swirly. They get to junior high and they won't want their heads in the toilet."

My stomach went squirmy. So *that's* what a swirly was. Yuck!

"We shouldn't talk about swirlies, though," Gordon said. "Bad luck. Might get one. Let's get back to Ernie's. You've got to see Ernie's Eatery, Ryan. You look hungry. Let's go get some food."

The thought of sitting down to a plateful of who-knows-what with Gordon at a restaurant called Ernie's Eatery was about as appealing to me as a swirly on the first day of junior high. "Uh . . . you go on," I said. "I need to baby-sit Justin and Ellie." I was scrounging, trying to come up with any excuse handy so I could go back to bed. "My parents are still asleep."

"Not anymore," came a cheerful voice from the top of the stairs. It was Dad. He came down, introduced himself to Gordon, saying how nice it was for me to have made a friend so fast. Before I knew it, he was putting three dollars into my hand, saying, "Go out for breakfast, Ryan. It's your first day in good ol' Macinburg. Celebrate!"

"Now you're talking!" Gordon said with his big grin. "Let's hit the feed bag!"

Hit the feed bag? Whatever happened to regular English? I did better with the kids in Arizona who spoke Spanish than with this strange Kentucky stuff.

Dad laughed as if Gordon was the wittiest kid in the world. "Yeah. You guys go *hit the feed bag* together."

I let out a big sigh. Between Gordon and my dad, it looked as if it might take less energy just to give in. "Okay," I said. But inside I was thinking, This had better be good.

CHAPTER 4

Slam Dunk Sky
Jumpers

Although it felt good to be riding my bike after a week in the car, doing it in Macinburg, Kentucky all but ruined the experience. Sure, the morning was bright and sunny and not nearly as hot as the day before. And there were flowers everywhere, and songbirds whooping it up in the trees—even mourning doves, just like in Arizona. And Gordon kept pointing things out—that this kid our age lived here, that a cool older kid named Telly Lewis lived there, and that Aaron Dexter's house was only a little bit farther down the road. And he said that Kentucky was a great state to live in if you like basketball. "People here go *crazy* over it!" And to top it all off, there was the hill just down Sycamore Street from our house. It was the best I'd ever gone down, with a great curve to go flying around at the bottom, then a bridge over a creek.

But it still wasn't Arizona. All the way to Ernie's Eatery, I couldn't stop thinking about the desert, prickly pear cactus in bloom, lizards on adobe walls, rocks to climb on, dirt not covered with grass.

Gordon didn't pick up on my mood, though. He just kept on grinning, riding along with his wiry hair standing up on end, talking about how I was going to love it here in "good ol' Macinburg." When we finally stopped in front of Ernie's Eatery, he acted especially proud. "Pretty nice, huh!" He beamed, pointing to what looked like nothing more than a freeway truck stop that had taken the wrong exit: parking lot, sidewalks all leading to glass double doors, lots of big windows, and a goofy neon sign with a chef tipping his puffy white hat and the words EAT HEARTY AT ERNIE'S EATERY! flashing below.

"They'll make a ton of money on sausage burgers, egg biscuits, grits, and coffee and stuff," Gordon said as if the idea were his. "I'm going to open up a restaurant just like it someday."

Why not run a funeral home and a restaurant at the same time? I started to say. You could call it Gordon's Mortuary, Home of the Mummy Burger. But Gordon had already parked his bike and was walking through the front door of Ernie's as if he owned the place.

Gordon ordered the $2.49 breakfast special: a sausage burger with cheese, grits, fries, and juice. I just got a Coke, thinking my stomach wasn't ready for anything gritty yet, or greasy. We sat down. Gordon munched away on his sausage burger, going on and on about how much money a restaurant like this could make—"No waitresses! Low overhead!"— when two boys walked in.

"Hey, Telly! Hey, Aaron!" Gordon called out.

As the boys walked over, Gordon whispered, "Remember? Telly Lewis and Aaron Dexter. We rode past their houses on the way here. They're both seventh-graders. Cool guys. Telly is a *great* basketball player, as good as any eighth-grader. He'll play for UK, I'll bet. Maybe even then on to the pros!"

That got my interest in a hurry. A *great* basketball player, huh? Good enough for the University of Kentucky, then the pros? Telly looked tall—*very* tall—even for a seventh-grader. Aaron did, too. I sat up as straight as I could, wondering just how great a basketball player Telly really was.

Right away Telly said, "Hey, check out my new shoes. Slam Dunk"—he flopped his hand over an imaginary rim like he was dunking the ball—"Sky Jumpers."

Gordon and I looked down at Telly's Slam Dunk Sky Jumpers. I'd seen them advertised on TV: the great All-Star pro Hoop Richardson sailing through the air with a pair on, acting like he didn't believe in gravity. He'd turned in midair and slam-dunked the ball behind his head without breaking a sweat. Sixty seconds of watching that kind of magic and you were ready to run right out and buy a pair. Slam Dunk Sky Jumpers. Surely they were the secret to Hoop's success.

"Got my pair just yesterday at Four-Star Sports," Telly said. He turned his new shoes this way and that, pointing out the great features that made you jump higher, run faster, shoot better, and look good while you were doing it.

"All the basketball guys are going to be wearing them like this," he said. He had them laced up halfway, with the tongue hanging out, and had bunched his white socks down around his ankles. "Pretty cool, huh?"

I found myself nodding. *Very* cool was more like it.

Gordon, I noticed, was nodding, too. "How much are they?" he asked.

I took a big swig of Coke. Good question.

"One twenty-four ninety-nine," Aaron offered.

At the sound of the price of a pair of Slam Dunk Sky Jumpers, Gordon sucked in a french fry whole.

I choked on the Coke still in my mouth, tried not to spit it all over Ernie's Eatery, and succeeded in blowing it out my nose instead.

Gordon didn't seem to notice that a good portion of the Coke spray went on his arm. "*Are we talking DOLLARS?*" he shouted at Aaron. "*One hundred twenty-four DOLLARS?*"

Aaron rolled his eyes. "No, ostrich feathers, dummy. Of course we're talking dollars. I'm going to get a pair today."

Coke bubbles were all over me, down my shirt, on my pants, and in my nose, tingling.

Telly laughed. "Who's your new friend, Gordon? Got some weird disease? Or does he think he's an elephant?"

Gordon recovered enough from the shock of hearing the price of a pair of Slam Dunk Sky Jumpers to notice the Coke on his arm.

"Yuck!" he said.

I grabbed a handful of paper napkins from the dispenser on the table. "I was just surprised at the price of those shoes," I mumbled. I could feel my face getting red.

Telly shook his head at Gordon and me. "Not cool. Definitely not cool." He leaned down and brushed a bit of Coke off his new Slam Dunk Sky Jumpers. "You guys are in for it. It's a whole different world in junior high, you know."

Sitting in Ernie's Eatery, covered with Coke bubbles from nose to toe, I found myself nodding. "Yeah," I said. "I've already gotten that idea."

Gordon and I biked slowly away from Ernie's after Telly and Aaron left. Gordon led the way, pedaling along the downtown Macinburg sidewalks. I followed, remembering when Patrick and I—the Desert Rats—used to ride out toward the canyon.

Gordon and I had gone just a few blocks when he braked hard, skidding to a stop.

With my brain in Arizona, I almost ran the rest of me into him. "Hey, watch it!" I said. "What did you do that for?"

Gordon pointed. "Look!"

I looked. We were in front of a store. Four-Star Sports, the sign said. And there in the center of the window display, sitting on top of a plastic pedestal for everyone to see, was a pair of Slam Dunk Sky Jumpers.

"Cool," I said.

Gordon nodded. "*Really* cool!" We got off our bikes and moved closer, pressing our noses to the glass.

"But one hundred twenty-four dollars and ninety-nine cents," Gordon said in a near whisper. "Plus tax. That's a *lot* of money."

I couldn't take my eyes off those Slam Dunk Sky
Jumpers. I imagined how they would look on me.
I'd wear them just like Telly, laced halfway up,
socks pushed down around my ankles. I'd look so
cool, no one would even think about giving me a
swirly on the first day of junior high. So cool I
wouldn't get picked on at all. So cool I'd play basketball with the seventh- and eighth-graders *and*
make the team. With those shoes on my feet, I'd be
so cool I'd end up playing for the University of
Kentucky, showing everybody what an Arizona boy
can do. Then I'd be off to the pros to play with
Hoop Richardson, just like Telly was going to do.
And all for only $124.99 plus tax. What a deal!

I almost laughed aloud, then stepped back from the
Four-Star Sports window. A deal? What was I thinking about? I was lucky if I had $20 in my little plastic
pig bank at home. Maybe $124.99 was nothing to
Telly or Aaron—their families must be loaded—or
maybe even for Gordon. (The way he talked about
getting rich, he probably had hundreds of dollars
saved up already.) But for me, $124.99 was the same
as a million.

Still, according to Telly, all the basketball players
would be wearing Slam Dunk Sky Jumpers. And
from the look on Gordon's face, pressed even flatter
now against the Four-Star Sports window, I could
tell that he was seriously considering parting with

some of his beloved money and buying a pair, too.

So it would be just me—short Ryan, the new kid in town—who would show up at junior high looking so totally uncool, so totally unbasketball, that I'd get a swirly before the first bell rang.

I stared at the Slam Dunk Sky Jumpers in the Four-Star Sports window, thinking that maybe $124.99 wasn't such a high price after all. Maybe it really was a deal. And maybe Mom and Dad could be convinced—if I explained everything a little better this time—to see it my way, too.

Maybe . . .

CHAPTER 5

Pleeeeease!

"**O**ne *hundred twenty-four dollars and ninety-nine cents?*" Dad said that night at dinner, a slice of pizza halfway to his mouth. "*For SHOES?*"

It was our first meal at the dining room table, which we had set up only minutes before. I looked across at him. "Special shoes," I offered.

He put the pizza back down on his plate and wiped the sweat from his forehead. (The air-conditioning still wasn't working.) "Shoes made out of gold, I guess."

I rolled my eyes. "Dad! They're Slam Dunk Sky Jumpers for junior high."

Mom shook her head. "I was afraid this was going to happen. Brand-name peer pressure."

"What's spear pressure?" Justin asked Ellie.

Ellie shook her head. "I don't know. Do you want your olives, Ryan?"

I gave her two olives off the slice of pizza on my plate, hoping that would keep her quiet. "But everybody will be wearing them," I explained.

"Everybody?" Dad asked.

"Well, a lot of people."

Mom let out a sigh. "We've spent most of our money getting here, Ryan. There are things that need to be done to the house, like fixing the air-conditioning." She glanced at Dad. "There's no money for expensive shoes, and even if there was, I don't think—"

"But Mom," I said, "this is *important.*"

Mom took a drink of iced tea. "We have to consider the whole family, Ryan," she said.

Ellie stuck an olive into her mouth, then smiled at me as she chewed. "Mmmm," she said. "I like olives."

Justin nodded. "Me, too." He looked over at my pizza slice.

I plucked another olive off my pizza and tossed it onto Justin's plate. "Eat and be quiet," I suggested, knowing good and well my advice was a waste of breath.

"Thank you," Justin said with a big grin.

"I know it's a lot of money," I said, turning back

to Dad. "But these are *really* great basketball shoes." This he'll understand, I thought. Dad loves basketball and played for Macinburg High School in the Kentucky State Tournament back in 1973.

Dad picked up his pizza slice and took a big bite. "You heard your mom," he said through the wad of dough. "Too expensive. We're not stockbrokers, you know."

Yeah, yeah. I'd already heard the speech a million times about how hard it is to make a living in the construction business.

"But you said coming to Kentucky we'd have more money," I reminded him.

"You don't get a check for a million dollars when you cross the state line, Ryan," he said. "It takes time, and *work*."

Here came the speech on hard work. I'd have to listen for the next ten minutes.

But Justin tapped me on the shoulder before Dad could get started and said, "If you say thank you to someone, don't they have to give you more olives?"

I quickly picked the rest of the olives off my pizza. "But I *need* a pair of Slam Dunk Sky Jumpers," I said, dividing the olives equally between the twins.

"Need?" asked Mom.

"A spaceman is coming to visit," Justin said. He grinned and stuck his finger through the hole in the sliced olive I'd given him. "Ellie and me heard it on the radio we found in the little closet."

Mom smiled at the twins. "Really!" she said, as if she believed every word of it. They both nodded, eyes wide with excitement.

"Yes, *need*," I insisted, trying to keep the conversation on track.

Ellie took a slurp of milk. "The spaceman is from another planet. His name is Quando."

"Pleeeeease," I begged, looking back and forth between Mom and Dad. "Just this once?"

"The spaceman wants to come live with us," Justin said. "Can he, Dad?"

"Sure," Dad said, and for a second I thought he was talking to me about Slam Dunk Sky Jumpers. But he was talking to Justin. "How big is this spaceman fellow?"

"*Pretty please,*" I said, a little louder this time. "I promise I'll never ask for anything like this again for as long as I live." I was beginning to feel desperate.

"Quando's not *too* big," Ellie said. "He could sleep in Ryan's room, on the top bunk."

"I don't have a bunk bed," I reminded her between clenched teeth. Anger began to creep up my spine. "We sold it in Arizona before we moved, remember?"

"Oh, that reminds me," Mom said. "There is an-

other family that has just moved here, too—the
Websters, from Mississippi. They live on Sycamore
Street, just like we do, only a couple blocks away,
right at the top of the hill. I met Mrs. Webster at the
grocery store. She was *so* friendly! I invited them
over for a barbecue tomorrow night."

"A party!" Ellie said.

"I love parties!" chimed in Justin. "Let's have lots
of soda pop and then we'll have a burping contest. I
like to burp, see!"

Justin let out a big belch. Dad laughed. Mom
said, "Now, Justin." But she was smiling when she
said it.

"I can burp good, too!" Ellie said. "You want to
hear?"

"*No!*" I shouted. Couldn't everybody see there
were more important things to talk about than burping? *"Just shut up, will you!"* Then I turned my anger
on Mom and Dad. *"You made me come here! You owe
me a pair of shoes!"*

The table went silent, and I knew that I'd blown
it. In my family, you can speak your mind, but in
no way are you supposed to shout it.

"To your room," Dad said in a calm but *very* firm
voice.

I tried to backpedal. "But . . . I didn't mean . . .
I just wanted to talk about the Slam Dunk Sky
Jumpers," I pleaded.

"Forget the shoes, Ryan," Mom said. "To your room."

"But it's not fair," I whined, forgetting that whining is useful only when you're the youngest in the family. Otherwise it just makes things worse.

"*Ryan*," Mom and Dad said at the same time, and I knew that it was hopeless. When they use that tone of voice, especially when they *both* use it and at the same time, any chance to argue a point is history.

I got up from the table and stalked toward my pink bedroom, glaring at the twins as I went.

Curtain climbers! Yard apes! Rug rats!

They both smiled and waved, a black olive stuck on the end of each finger.

CHAPTER 6

Ninety-Nine Dollars and Ninety-Nine Cents

The next morning, Dad unboxed the TV and hooked it up to cable. I turned the set on, fished around for a station, and what was the first thing I saw? You guessed it: NBA All-Star Hoop Richardson and that ad for Slam Dunk Sky Jumpers.

"Hey, Dad, come see this," I called out, thinking that maybe if he witnessed a pair of shoes like that in action, he might change his mind.

"Shoes don't make the ballplayer, Ryan," was all he said after watching for two seconds. Then he went back to working on the air conditioner.

Disgusted, I turned the TV off and wandered outside to shoot a few baskets. The hoop mounted on the garage was a good one, but I couldn't seem to hit, especially like Hoop Richardson. I was sure it was because this rim was in Kentucky, not Arizona, and my shoes were discount bargains, not Slam Dunk Sky Jumpers. So I went for a bike ride down the Sycamore Street hill, around the curve, and over the bridge. It felt so good to go fast that I did it again. At the bottom of my second run, I saw Telly and Aaron skipping rocks in the creek, now *both* wearing Slam Dunk Sky Jumpers.

Everywhere I looked, there were my shoes. It was obvious. I had to have a pair. *I had* to.

When I got home, I offered to help unpack boxes —in that stuffy, hot old house, no less. As we worked, Dad still kept saying things like "That's just too much money for a pair of shoes." And Mom kept agreeing. "*Entirely* too much." I was beginning to get really depressed.

Then luck turned my way. Dad had finally gotten the air conditioner going. We were all standing around the vent saying "Aaaaah," enjoying the cool air, when Gordon came rushing into the house— without knocking, of course—and yelled, "They're on sale! Slam Dunk Sky Jumpers are on sale at Four-Star Sports!"

Gordon and I jumped on our bikes and flew down the Sycamore Street hill, around the curve, over the creek bridge. Sure enough, there they were in the display window of Four-Star Sports, Slam Dunk

Sky Jumpers, still sitting high and mighty on that plastic pedestal, but now with a big sign that said, *One Week Only! $99.99*

The lady in the shoe department, Mrs. Marcosa, said that at that price they were going fast. "The sale is just on the sizes we have in stock. No layaways. Better hurry."

I checked the boxes of Slam Dunk Sky Jumpers she had stacked neatly on the counter. Only one had my size—seven—printed on it.

Gordon had pulled a small black book out of his back pocket and was running his finger down a column of figures, studying it carefully. "My bankbook," he said when I asked.

That did it. Now Gordon was going to buy a pair. I rode home and told Mom and Dad about the sale.

And they finally gave in. Dad broke down first and said, "Okay, okay. We'll give you the money we were going to spend on a new pair—forty dollars. If you want to earn the rest, if that's how you really want to spend your time and your money, go ahead."

Then Mom let out a sigh and said, "I guess you're old enough to make your own decisions, Ryan. Just try to be responsible about them, okay?"

"*Yes!*" I yelled over my shoulder. I was already halfway out of the living room, headed for the land of pink to check my own little bank account. "YA-HOO!"

I tossed my plastic piggy bank on the bed, yanked the rubber stopper from its belly, and dumped my savings out on the blanket.

"Twenty-one forty-five," I announced to myself a moment later. "With the forty dollars from Mom and Dad, plus my savings, I only need . . ." I got a piece of paper and started subtracting: "Ninety-nine ninety-nine minus twenty-one forty-five . . . minus forty . . ."

Then I remembered the sales tax Mom and Dad would have had to pay on forty-dollar shoes. How much was it in Kentucky?

"Six percent," Dad said, rolling his eyes when I reminded him that they would have to pay that at a store anyway. "But don't forget that you have to pay the sales tax on the entire ninety-nine ninety-nine."

It took a few tries and Mom's calculator, but I finally figured it all out. The total on the Slam Dunk Sky Jumpers, including 6 percent sales tax, would be $105.99. Mom and Dad would throw in $42.40 altogether. That and my $21.45 added up to $63.85—which, subtracted from $105.99, meant that I only had to come up with $42.14. Those Slam Dunk Sky Jumpers were beginning to look downright cheap!

I was still sitting on my bed, recounting and calculating, thinking of ways that I could earn $42.14, when Mom knocked on the door and said, "Come on out, Ryan. The Websters are here."

Oh yeah, the barbecue. I carefully put my money back in Piggy, then walked out into the living room to find myself looking straight into the biggest, greenest pair of eyes I'd ever seen in my life.

Girl eyes.

"Hi there," the girl said, and for the first time I thought that a southern accent might be a beautiful thing. Those two ordinary, regular old words—*hi* and *there*—suddenly sounded smooth and warm and perfect, like a rock you'd want to add to your collection.

Then the girl said, "My name is Bobbie Jo." She smiled at me, and I could swear I felt my heart skip one complete beat.

CHAPTER 7

Fried Ham, Cheese, and Bologna

Bobbie Jo's family, I quickly found out, had moved from a place called Hattiesburg, Mississippi, to Macinburg. "Frog hopped" was the way Bobbie Jo put it. Her dad worked for some company that seemed to think living in one place for more than a year was bad for your health. "I've been in seven different schools since kindergarten," she said.

I smiled, thinking more of Bobbie Jo every minute. Not only did she have those incredible green eyes and a pretty smile, but she also knew what it was like to be ripped away from everything you know, forced into a place where you don't want to be, faced with swirlies and weird neighbors with dogs name Colonel and junior high school one year too soon. She understood how I felt.

Wrong. "I love getting into a new town," she said. "New house. New school. New friends. Moving is *great!* Don't you think so, Ryan?"

Everybody looked at me.

"Well . . . uh," I said, suddenly feeling like a spineless worm for ever complaining.

Which I didn't like one bit.

Which I blamed on Bobbie Jo.

Suddenly her eyes didn't seem so green, her smile so pretty, her southern accent so warm and smooth and perfect. What did she know, anyway? She'd moved so many times, she'd probably left her brain in the ladies' room at some rest stop. Now that I'd taken a good look, she was two cards short of a deck: pea-brained, pug-nosed, and, to top it all off, not from Arizona!

But the twins thought Bobbie Jo was the best thing to come along since dinosaurs. She talked to them, asking questions about starting kindergarten, their stuffed animals, and if they liked their hamburgers with onions or not. Before I knew it, the three of them were sitting in a little circle out on the back lawn, chatting away like they'd known each other for centuries. I acted like I was helping Dad and Mr. Webster light the charcoal, but I was really listening to what they said.

Ellie told Bobbie Jo all about the gila woodpecker that pestered us in Arizona. It used to steal dry food from our neighbor's cat's dish and stash it in our pants pockets when the laundry was hung out to dry. We found it when we got dressed in the morning. "It took us a *long* time to figure out how that food got there," Ellie said, as if that was surprising.

Justin told Bobbie Jo that he thought Dad's face felt just like a cactus in the morning before he shaved. "I used to rub it and say, 'Daddy's cactus! Daddy's cactus!' "

Bobbie Jo laughed, acting like these were the best stories ever told. I shook my head. Moving a lot obviously chewed up a person's mind.

Of course, the twins got around to telling Bobbie Jo all about their "space radio" and Quando's visit.

Bobbie Jo went on as if she believed them, saying, "Wow! I've never met an alien before, but I'd be happier than a flea at a dog show if I did!"

The twins lit up at this lie. Ellie said, "I like the way you talk." Justin said, "Me, too!"

Bobbie Jo laughed even harder. "It's a special gift they give you when you grow up in the South. But outsiders can learn how if they work real hard at it. You want to give it a try?"

The twins bounced up and down. "Yeah! Yeah!"

Which is about when I checked out of their dippy conversation. I had more important things to do than

watch my brother and sister practice saying "Hi,
y'all" and "That's a who'd-a-thought-it" and "It's so
hot out, the tomatoes mighty near gonna stew on the
vine." Instead, I had to concentrate on how I was
going to earn $42.14 before the One-Week-Only
Sale on Slam Dunk Sky Jumpers ended at Four-Star
Sports. Maybe Bobbie Jo thought she could just
float right into junior high like a boat on the Mississippi River, but she'd find out different soon
enough.

I looked over at her as she switched from fairly
stupid speech lessons to completely dumb songs. As
I was soon to hear—over and over and over again—
there were more idiotic tunes in the world than "On
Top of Spaghetti."

"Fried ham, fried ham, cheese, and bologna,"
Bobbie Jo and Justin and Ellie all sang, as if the
whole neighborhood was dying to hear.

"And after the macaroni,
  We'll have onions, pickles, and peppers,
  And then we'll have some more fried ham,
  FRIED HAM! FRIED HAM!"

Good grief!

CHAPTER 8

Junior High Insurance

I set to work as soon as possible earning the money for my Slam Dunk Sky Jumpers.

Dad paid me two dollars to clean out the basement and three more to wash the station wagon—so dirty, a pig in mud would have looked cleaner—then wax it. Mr. Jackson, who lived next to us, hired me to dig up all the weeds along his rock wall. An old lady down the block said she'd pay me to water her flower garden while she was gone for two days to visit her son in some town that sounded dangerous. "Hazard, Kentucky," she called it. Mom paid me a dollar to scrub under the kitchen sink.

I worked like crazy, not even taking time off when Gordon invited me to go swimming on Tuesday at

Wrennington Lake. I saved everything I made, every penny. I didn't buy one pop or candy bar, not a single pack of baseball cards, not even a sausage burger at Ernie's Eatery. It all went into Piggy. I counted and recounted at the end of each day.

I dropped by Four-Star Sports each day, too, and checked up on my size-seven Slam Dunk Sky Jumpers. Mrs. Marcosa got kind of tired of pulling them out of the box and showing them to me, but she still smiled and said, "Sale's on until Saturday! Get the money and they're yours!"

Eleven dollars. Thirteen fifty. Seventeen, then nineteen. By my count, first thing Thursday morning I was twenty-two dollars and seventy-five cents closer to my goal. Including my savings and the money Mom and Dad were pitching in, I needed only $19.39 more!

But I was out of jobs. I asked Mom and Dad for more work. But they said, "Sorry, not right now." Which made me mad. They'd gotten good jobs for themselves and now had run out of anything for me. I went to ask the folks on my block again.

No help there, either. Nothing.

I branched out, covering the entire neighborhood, knocking on every door, asking, nearly begging. The sale on Slam Dunk Sky Jumpers ended in just three days!

At Bobbie Jo's house, though, I hesitated on the front steps, thinking maybe I wasn't that desperate. She'd visited the twins twice more since the cook-out, telling them stories and teaching them songs, listening to their never ending Quando stories. Just having her in the house made me feel weird and confused inside. I'd find myself staring at her, wanting to see those green eyes sparkle, that smile of hers. But then she'd make a comment about the way I chew my food—"Like a cow!"—or talk about how excited she was to be going to junior high, and I'd want her to leave. Who knew what she'd say if I told her why I was looking for a job? So I turned away from Bobbie Jo's, deciding I'd hunt for aluminum cans to cash in instead.

But before I'd gotten five feet, Bobbie Jo's dad opened the front door, coffee cup in hand, and said, "Well now! Look who's here!"

"None other than Ryan O'Keefe," Bobbie Jo said as she came out onto the porch behind him. "What are you up to?"

I felt like I'd been caught doing something wrong, even though I hadn't, but couldn't think of a thing to say. "Uh . . . well . . . ummmm," I mumbled like my mouth was stuck in neutral.

Bobbie Jo smiled, and those green eyes flashed. Which made me feel all the more confused and flustered, until I finally just blurted out the truth. "I'm looking for a job so I can buy a pair of Slam Dunk Sky Jumpers for junior high."

Bobbie Jo laughed—a big, in-your-face kind of laugh. "Slam Dunk Sky Jumpers?" she said.

I went straight from confused and flustered to really mad. I was just about to say, "Yeah! So what, mudbrain?"

But her dad put an end to that. "Come to think of it," he said, "I need some work done in the garden. There are bushes that have to be dug out, rocks moved, an old fence torn down. I haven't got the time right now. Too much going on at work. And Bobbie Jo is helping inside unpacking boxes. There's lots of weeding I'd like to get done, too. I could pay you fifteen . . . no, it's a big job . . . I could pay you twenty dollars if you do it all. You got a strong back, Ryan?"

I jumped forward. "Yes, sir! And I can start right away!" Twenty dollars would put me over the top!

Bobbie Jo snickered, but I decided to ignore her, pretend I didn't hear her insults, didn't know she was there. Even when she followed her dad and me back to the garage and stood too close as he explained everything that needed to be done.

I kept ignoring her all the rest of the day Thursday, then all day Friday, too. Whenever she came around, I just kept to the job, making sure she saw that I was a hard worker and how much I knew about doing things right.

It was almost dark on Friday evening when I finally finished. My hands were blistered, and my arms and back ached, but Mr. Webster paid me—a crisp, green twenty-dollar bill—and I had enough money, even a few cents extra . . . sixty-one! First thing in the morning, I'd be counting it out in front of Mrs. Marcosa, and those Slam Dunk Sky Jumpers would me mine, all mine!

That night I could hardly get to sleep. I lay in bed, looking out the window. Lightning bugs, so different from anything we had in Arizona, flashed yellow on the other side of the glass. When I finally did doze off, I dreamed that I showed up on the first day of school not only without a pair of Slam Dunk Sky Jumpers on but without anything else on, either.

What a nightmare! All the kids laughed, especially Bobbie Jo, as I tried to hide in a garbage can.

I woke up in a cold sweat Saturday morning and jumped out of bed. I scarfed down a bagel and cream cheese. Then I wrote Mom and Dad a note saying I'd had breakfast and was out for a bike ride. I flew down the Sycamore Street hill and rode hard toward Four-Star Sports, even though it was still a full hour before they opened.

But even though I was the first one in the door at

8:30, my size-seven Slam Dunk Sky Jumpers were already gone. "Sold that pair just before closing yesterday," Mrs. Marcosa said. "I couldn't hold them. I told you before: no layaways on sale items."

"But . . . but . . . ," I stuttered.

"We'll have a new shipment in by Monday," Mrs. Marcosa said. "There will be several pairs of size seven, I'm sure. They won't be on sale, though. The price will be back up to one twenty-four ninety-nine plus tax." She checked a little chart she had taped to the cash register. "That'll be one thirty-two forty-nine altogether."

$132.49. The figures hit me like a fist in the stomach. Even with the $20 Mr. Webster had paid me, I only had $106.60.

"I'm sorry," Mrs. Marcosa said, and I could tell she really meant it, "but you were too late. That's a fact."

A fact. You can't explain or argue or beg away a fact. And the fact was that all of a sudden instead of having sixty-one cents extra, I was $25.89 short. And school started in just three days—on Tuesday. Where could I get $25.89 in that amount of time? *How?*

I had no idea.

*   *   *

The Sycamore Street hill seemed steeper, the air hotter and more humid, and Macinburg, Kentucky, even farther from Arizona than ever before as I rode home.

I tried to cheer myself up by shooting a few baskets. I still couldn't hit, though. Of course not—no Slam Dunk Sky Jumpers.

I gave up and went into the garage, only to find the twins happily drawing on the box we'd moved the refrigerator in.

"It's going to be our spaceship," Justin said.

Ellie nodded. "Yeah, so we can go to the moon and meet Quando! He called us on the radio again and said he doesn't want to come to Earth. There's too much pollution and stuff like that here. So we're going to meet him on the moon instead!"

"Sleepy Bear and Hippo are going, too," Justin added. He put his crayon down and inspected the spaceship. "Where should we put the flashlight, Ryan? We need to put one on, like a car headlight."

"You always have good ideas," Ellie said to me. "You always help us."

"Well, not today," I said. "I'm sick of all this spaceman stuff. Don't you guys ever think about anything else?"

I went into the house. Mom was unpacking boxes, Dad messing with a door that wouldn't shut right.

Dad whistled while he worked. Mom hummed along. It was disgusting. How could everybody be happy in a dumpy house so far from home?

"I'll start painting your room next week," Mom said. "I got the paint already. It's that desert color you wanted." She smiled, as if a light brown bedroom was all I needed. "It's a beautiful day out today, isn't it? How was your bike ride?"

I wanted to shout at her and Dad, "IT WAS AWFUL! THEY SOLD MY SHOES! TAKE ME BACK TO ARIZONA!" But I poured myself a glass of lemonade, then went to the front porch steps to sit and think.

As soon as I got settled, though, Gordon walked up with Colonel. "Howdy-ho," he said, and grinned. "Notice anything different?"

I looked down. On Gordon's feet were a brand-new pair of Slam Dunk Sky Jumpers.

"Junior high insurance," he said. "I decided it was worth it and broke into my savings account while the sale was still on."

I stood up, then quickly moved down the front steps for a closer look at Gordon's new shoes. "What size are they?" I asked.

Gordon grinned as big as I'd ever seen him grin. "Seven!" he said. "Haw! Perfecto fit!"

CHAPTER 9

The Wonderful Shade of a New Dollar Bill

"But . . . but . . . ," I stuttered, "that's the same size I wear! I was looking at them when we were at Four-Star Sports. Remember?"

Gordon's eyes went wide with surprise. "No. I didn't notice. We wear the same size? Really?" He looked down at his feet, then at mine. "I've got small feet, I reckon. Or you must have pretty big ones for somebody so short."

Right then I came within an inch of slugging Gordon for calling me short, not to mention for having my shoes. But he saw the look in my eyes and quickly added, "Long feet means you're going to get a lot bigger soon. You'll end up taller than me, I can tell—probably six foot six, maybe even taller."

Dad had said the same thing many times. "You're like a puppy. You'll grow into those feet, then look out!" It always made me feel better. I nodded at Gordon. "Yeah, I will be tall."

Gordon grinned, obviously relieved. He leaned down and petted Colonel. "You'll make a *great* basketball player someday, Ryan. You'll be as good as Telly!"

A little smile crept onto my face at the added compliment. It was true. I would be a great ballplayer someday: as good as Telly—even better.

The little smile vanished, though, as I looked again at my shoes on Gordon's feet. I had the sudden urge to knock him down and take what was rightfully mine. But instead I said, "Gotta go," and walked back into the house real quick before I changed my mind.

Gordon and Colonel followed me, though. "Feel like I'm floating in the air with these Slam Dunk Sky Jumpers on," Gordon said as we walked across the living room. "Haw! I guess that's worth all that money, huh?"

I didn't answer, just kept on toward my bedroom. Maybe Mom would spot Colonel and shoo him *and* his owner out, too.

No such luck. No parents in sight. Gordon and Colonel followed me past the stairs and down the little hall.

"Hey! Pepto-Bismol walls!" Gordon exclaimed when he stepped into my pink bedroom.

"Glad you like them," I muttered as sarcastically as I could.

Gordon laughed. "Haw! Can you sleep, or does all this pink keep you awake at night?"

I sat down on my bed and glared at him.

Colonel started nosing around. Just like his dog, Gordon started nosing, too, checking out the few things I'd taken the time to put out on my dresser, my shelves, the bedside table.

Gordon stopped short when he came to Fang's terrarium on a little table by the window. He craned his neck, keeping his distance, peering in. "I'll bet there are tarantulas and rattlesnakes everywhere in Arizona, huh?" he said. He spotted Fang under his rock. "Poisonous things."

How dumb. He really thought that was what Arizona was like.

Being a desert lover, I wanted to set Gordon straight right then and there. He'd been watching too many movies. The Sonoran desert wasn't just sand and rocks. There were lots and lots of great plants: palo verde trees with lime-green bark, mesquite trees, and all kinds of cactuses—or *cacti*, like Dad wanted me to say when talking about more than one.

I liked the saguaro cacti best of all. They're big

and tall. The biggest in the world, near Gila Bend, is 57 feet, 11¾ inches tall! Some of them have arms that look like they're waving at you, and all of them have little ridges with spines. But the skin between the spines is green and smooth to the touch. And when the wind blows, the spines make a neat noise, a soft whistle.

I had caught Fang near a saguaro. He wasn't a deadly monster. He was all I had left of the desert, my favorite place in the whole wide world. How did I explain that to Gordon? How did I tell him what it was really like?

I decided not to. Gordon was wearing my shoes. He didn't deserve to know.

Gordon leaned a little closer to Fang's terrarium and asked, "What do you feed it?"

Good grief! There I was thinking about how much Fang meant to me, and I'd been so busy trying to earn money to buy a pair of Slam Dunk Sky Jumpers, I'd forgotten to feed him. Sure, tarantulas can go days without food, but Fang was due . . . *over*due.

I jumped up and ran into the backyard. Gordon and Colonel followed, Gordon saying, "Hey! Where're you going?"

I ignored him and began to rustle around in the bushes until I saw a cricket jump. Colonel lunged for it, but I nabbed it first (I'm a good cricket catcher).

Colonel barked. I cupped the cricket in two hands and rushed back inside. Gordon and Colonel trailed behind me. "You're going to feed your spider one of *those?*" Gordon asked as I lifted the screen off Fang's terrarium.

"Yep," I said, and dropped the cricket in.

In a flash, Fang rushed at the cricket and grabbed it. Gordon jumped back. Colonel let out a soft whine. "Whoa!" Gordon said with a nervous smile. "He was a hungry critter, huh?"

"Sucks the blood right out of them," I said, hoping to make him squirm.

Gordon moved closer as my spider sunk his fangs into the cricket, finishing it off. "Wow!" he said. "People would pay money to see that."

Colonel put his front paws up on the table and looked into Fang's terrarium, as if he smelled money, too.

I shook my head. Money, money, money. Show Gordon a desert animal doing what it does naturally, and all he sees is a cash register filling up with—

"Hey, wait a minute!" I said to myself. I watched Gordon lean even closer to the terrarium. "Wow!" he kept saying. "Just like a real-life horror movie."

A smile crept onto my face. People love horror movies. And they pay money to see them. I still needed twenty-five dollars and eighty-nine cents to get a pair of Slam Dunk Sky Jumpers at the regular price. Mrs. Marcosa said she'd have some more size sevens in by Monday. It was still early on Saturday. That meant I had almost three days. . . .

I looked again at Gordon, whose eyes were glued to the action in the terrarium as if it were a miniature movie screen. He was watching my wonderful spider, Fang, who to me was beginning to look sort of green—not sickly green, but the wonderful green shade of a brand-new dollar bill.

CHAPTER 10

Think Business

Although Gordon didn't say anything else about having bought the last pair of size-seven Slam Dunk Sky Jumpers, I got the feeling he felt a little bad about it after all. When I told him my idea of making money by charging kids to see Fang, he said, "You bet!" He helped me set up a card table in front of the house, under the big oak tree. He lettered a sign that read, SEE THE TARANTULA! ONLY 25 CENTS! and taped it to the front of the table. He even held the door for me as I carried out Fang's terrarium.

"Thanks," I said. Now that I had a way to get those Slam Dunk Sky Jumpers, I wasn't so mad anymore. It would be fun to show off Fang and make money at the same time.

"This could be even better than Ernie's Eatery!" Gordon exclaimed. He raced over to his house and came back with a couple of folding chairs. "We'll just sit here," he said, setting them up in the shade behind the card table, "and before you can say knick-knack-paddy-whack, that good old money will come rolling home!"

I smiled. He was right. I'd probably have the $25.89 before closing time at Four-Star Sports. Just wait.

Wait is exactly what we did, and wait, and wait, and wait. Three hours went by—three hot, humid August hours in which Colonel finally gave up and wandered home—and no one even gave us a second look.

Except the twins. They rode up on their bicycles, Sleepy Bear and Hippo stuffed in the handlebar baskets, singing another stupid song Bobbie Jo had taught them, this one about pigs. "Two of 'em small, and two so tall, they danced all night at the pig town ball . . ."

I said, "You guys need to leave. You're interfering with business."

Justin looked up and down the vacant sidewalk. "I don't see any business."

Ellie got off her bike and walked over to Fang. "Me, neither."

Gordon rolled his eyes. "I have to put up with

this kind of stuff at home," he said. "J.T. comes into my room and bugs me all the time."

I nodded at Gordon, then said to the twins, "Get lost. You're in the way."

Ellie said, "We just came to tell you that Quando sent us a new message on the radio. He's getting closer to the moon."

Gordon let out a sharp laugh.

I made my voice sound tough. "What do I have to do, call NASA to prove no space alien is going to meet you on the moon?"

"What's NASA?" Justin wanted to know.

Ellie put her hands on her hips. "Bobbie Jo believes us."

I said, "That figures."

Justin and Ellie both went over to Fang's terrarium and peered inside.

"Come on, you guys," I said, growing more frustrated. "We're trying to make some *money*."

They ignored me and kept looking at Fang.

Just then, a car turned the corner and pulled over toward the curb. "Our first customer!" I said.

But as the car came to a stop, I could see that it was Bobbie Jo and her mom. Bobbie Jo rolled down the passenger's side window and leaned out. "We just stopped to see what you guys were up to," she said, her green eyes sparkling. As I watched her read Gordon's sign, I found myself thinking that she was pretty in a different way from movie stars or models on TV. She was pretty in a way that I couldn't describe but that, I had to admit, I liked . . . a lot. Her eyes and smile were only part of it. There was something about the way she tucked her hair behind her ear, how she tilted her head a little to one side when she was thinking, and how—

"Some people will do anything to make money, huh?" Bobbie Jo said.

I couldn't believe it. Here I had been thinking about how pretty Bobbie Jo was, and then *this!* I felt myself getting red in the face—first from feeling mushy over a girl, then from anger. I wanted to say something back to Bobbie Jo, to show her I could be just as much a smart-mouth as she was. But I couldn't think of a thing to say.

The twins had no such problem, though. "Bobbie Jo!" Justin yelled as if he hadn't seen her for three hundred years. Ellie, too. "Bobbie Jo!" They ran over to the car and told her the latest news from Quando. She listened as if every word was much too important to miss. She patted each of the twins on the head, then smiled as they got on their bikes and rode happily off, singing, "Two of 'em small, and two so tall, they danced all night at the pig town ball . . ."

Bobbie Jo looked back at Fang, the sign, and me. "Bye-bye!" she said, as friendly as could be, then rolled up her window. But I could see her shaking her head as her mom drove away.

It wasn't until Bobbie Jo was out of sight that I thought to call after her, "Bye-bye to you, too, Miss Know-It-All."

Gordon added, "Yeah! Miss Know-*Nothing*-At-All."

I nodded. "Miss Know-ABSOLUTELY-Nothing-At-All."

We both grinned and were so busy giving each other high-fives that we hardly noticed the boy who rode up on his bike and went over to look at Fang.

"A *real* customer this time!" Gordon said.

I jumped out of my folding chair and walked to where the kid was peering down into Fang's terrarium. He looked to be about a third-grader, definitely old enough to have a quarter in his pocket.

"Want to see the tarantula?" I asked.

"Already have," the kid said. "He's just sitting there. Big deal." Then he jumped on his bike and rode off.

"Hey!" I called after him. "You forgot to pay!"

But he was already up to full speed, heading down the Sycamore Street hill.

"Aw!" I said, plopping back down in my chair. I threw up my hands in disgust. "I'm never going to get those Slam Dunk Sky Jumpers like this!"

Gordon didn't answer. He tucked his feet under

his chair—as if that would hide the fact that he had on my shoes—and rubbed his chin like he was thinking.

Suddenly he blurted out, "We've just been going about this all wrong! Why didn't I think of it before? You've got to hook people in if you want to make money. You've got to make them think you're giving them something really special." He hit himself on the forehead with the palm of his hand. "Sure! We just need to boogey things up a bit! We need better advertising!"

Gordon jumped from his chair and tore the sign he had made off the card table, flipped it over, and began to write with the marker: ONCE-IN-A-LIFETIME CHANCE! SEE FANG THE TERRIBLE TARANTULA! SPECIAL PRICE! JUST 25 CENTS. He looked down the street and said, "Watch this!"

Another boy—this time a little younger, maybe a second-grader—was headed our way on a bike.

Gordon stood on the curb and held the sign up so the kid couldn't help seeing it. He waved the kid over, saying, "Only a quarter! What a deal! Step right up!"

Before I knew it, the boy had indeed stepped right up, and I was holding twenty-five cents in my hand.

"See? I told you so!" Gordon said after the boy rode off. He slapped his thigh. "You've got to think business."

I put the quarter on the card table and pushed it away. "But Fang isn't terrible," I said, and started to explain a spider's life in the desert.

Gordon wasn't interested in desert details, though. "We're on a roll now, Ryan!" he said. "Haw! I can feel it!" He grabbed the marker again and added to the sign, BIGGEST SPIDER IN CAPTIVITY! DANGER! DANGER! Then he started for the curb again. A car was headed our way.

"Fang is not the biggest spider in captivity!" I said. "And he's not dangerous, either!"

Gordon held the sign up toward the car as if he hadn't heard.

"That sign is wrong!" I said, and to prove it, I walked straight over to Fang's terrarium and took the screen off. "You think he's so dangerous! Watch this!"

Gordon turned. His eyes went wide with fear as I stuck my hand into the glass tank. "Don't!" he yelled.

Fang moved toward my fingers.

"Ryan! Get your hand out of there!"

I turned my palm up and gently moved my hand toward Fang. He walked right up onto my fingers. "See?" I said as I lifted Fang out and held him toward Gordon.

Gordon backed up a step, a look of shock on his face. He tilted his head and stared at Fang, then at me, then back at Fang. Slowly, his expression changed from shock to wonder. "Yeah, I see," he said as he burst into a big grin, his eyebrows going all lop-sided. "I see that people will sure as shootin' pay to see you do *that*." And he quickly added to the sign, EXTRA ATTRACTION FREE! WATCH RYAN PICK UP THE KILLER SPIDER! "This will *really* bring them in!"

"But it's all a lie," I said, lowering Fang into his terrarium, as if that were the end of that.

Gordon walked over to the card table and picked up the quarter I'd pushed away. "No, it's business," he said. He slipped the quarter into my shirt pocket. "If you want to make money, you've got to think business."

As if to prove him right, the second-grade boy was coming back up the street, and he had another kid with him who was about fourth-grade size.

"See, I told you it was a tarantula," the younger boy said to the older one.

The older boy looked at the sign, then at me, and asked, "Is that thing really dangerous?"

I looked over at Gordon. He mouthed the words *Think business.*

I looked back at the two boys and thought about the Slam Dunk Sky Jumpers. I was going to have to make money fast if I was going to get them. Business seemed the only way, and here it was staring me in the face.

"Can you really pick it up?" the older boy wanted to know.

I walked over to Fang's terrarium. Slowly and dramatically, I lifted the screen off and set it on the card table. "He's dangerous all right," I said. "A real killer." I motioned the boys closer. "But for just a quarter—each—I'll pick him up anyway. Honest, I will."

CHAPTER 11

The Fiercest Spider in the World

The next day after church, I ate lunch as fast as I could. Dad told me to slow down, to stop taking such big bites. He kept talking about the remodeling job he was starting the next day in a nearby town, "over in Booneburg." He was going to go look at it again, even though it was Sunday, to double-check his materials list.

Mom worried that she wasn't going to get all the unpacking and painting done before she had to start her bank job. "But I'll get to your room, Ryan. Don't worry."

Justin and Ellie had found out from Mom that they would have to have shots before they could start kindergarten.

"It's a law," Ellie said.

Justin said, "We go to the doctor's office tomorrow."

They both looked nervous and wanted to know if the shots would hurt less if they shut their eyes and held their breath. "Did that help you, Ryan? Did you cry or run away?"

"I don't remember," I said, even though I really did. I was in a hurry, and despite everything that was going on, managed to get my meal down in record time.

It took a bit of explaining to Mom and Dad—especially Mom, who kept shaking her head and saying, "I don't know about this Ryan"—but by 1:30 I had their permission to set up our family camping tent in the front yard. I put Fang's terrarium inside on the card table, then covered it with a cloth napkin.

I made two new signs, adding the words DEADLY POISONOUS and a drawing of Fang to what Gordon had already written. (Fang *was* deadly poisonous . . . if you were a cricket.) Then I thumbtacked the signs on either side of a telephone pole, so people would be sure to see them no matter which way they came down Sycamore Street.

Counting the three quarters I'd made the day before, I'd figured on Mom's calculator that I needed only $25.14 more to get my Slam Dunk Sky Jumpers. With my great spider show, it would be no sweat. I went inside to get into a costume: a T-shirt with Fang drawn on the front and a black bow tie and straw hat from the twins' dress-up box.

"Step right up!" I yelled as I ran back out onto the front lawn. I waved my hat over my head. "See Fang the killer tarantula! Fiercest spider in the world! Feeding time in only ten minutes! Witness death for only a quarter! Dangerous spider handling, too! Step right up!"

It took a few minutes—enough time for me to start getting a little hoarse—but finally a boy walked around the corner onto Sycamore Street, heard me yelling, and came to investigate.

And just like that I had a customer. "Greatest show *anywhere!*" I yelled at two girls on bikes as I took the boy's quarter and showed him where to sit on the tent floor. "Front-row seats still available!"

The girls rode up, looked at the sign and the tent, then asked if they had time to go get their friends.

"Hurry! Hurry!" I yelled. "Seats are going fast! Tell *everyone* you meet."

The girls went riding off. Minutes later Telly and Aaron showed up (both wearing their Slam Dunk Sky Jumpers, of course).

"What's all this about a big spider?" Telly wanted

to know. "Is this for real, or are you just going to blow more Coke bubbles out of your nose?"

I forced a laugh. "That was my other show," I said, trying to act more confident than I felt with two big seventh-graders in my front yard. "This is a cool show, and it only costs a quarter."

Aaron frowned. "I'm not going to pay a quarter just to see a spider. This looks like a little kids' thing to me."

I acted like I didn't hear him and took a quarter from a smaller boy I ushered into the tent.

"You're afraid of spiders, that's all," I heard Telly tease Aaron.

"I am not!" Aaron shot back.

Telly laughed. "Then go in and pick it up."

Aaron squirmed around a bit. I knew how he felt—the same way I did when I was teased for being short. "It takes special training and skill to pick up a tarantula," I said, making my voice as grown-up and official as I could.

"Hear that?" Aaron said to Telly. "It takes special training."

Telly grinned at him. "I still think you're too scared of the thing to even go in."

Aaron scowled. "I'm not scared, and I'll prove it." He fished in his pocket and pulled out some change, then counted two quarters into my hand. "Let's go see the kiddie show," he said, and he and Telly went in.

Gordon came across Sycamore Street grinning like he does. "Hey! Now you're playing it smart!" he said, slapping me on the back. "I'd say you need a business partner."

As much as I appreciated Gordon's good ideas, I did *not* need a business partner. Partners take half the money. That would mean I'd have to make twice as much to get my Slam Dunk Sky Jumpers.

"Since I helped get things off the ground, you know," Gordon said, his grin still cranked up full blast.

"Uh . . . I'll let you in for free," I offered.

Gordon's grin dropped. "Is that all?"

"It's the best I can do," I tried to explain. The two girls that had come by earlier came running back with another girl. All three paid and went inside. "School starts Tuesday," I said to Gordon. "You've got your shoes already."

Gordon looked down at his Slam Dunk Sky Jumpers. "Well . . . I guess so. Still, this was kind of my idea, you know."

"And I really appreciate it," I said, showing him to a seat in the tent. "Really I do."

Think business, Gordon had said. That's what I was doing. Giving up a place in the tent to a nonpaying customer was the same as giving up a quarter.

The twins had come over to see what was going on. They were standing outside the tent, each holding a pair of toy binoculars.

"Spaceman binoculars," Ellie said, holding them up for me to see.

Justin looked at me through his. "Quando said over the radio that he doesn't like fried ham, or cheese and bologna." He turned the binoculars toward the tent. "So we're on the lookout for other food for him."

I tried to ignore them. *Think business*, I reminded myself.

Ellie looked into the tent through her binoculars. "Are you going to feed Fang, Ryan?"

I noticed a kid watching from across the street. He looked curious enough to cough up a quarter. "Yep," I said to the twins as I waved him over. "Lots of blood and gore."

"Can we watch?" Ellie asked.

The kid started across the street, digging into his pocket as he came. "For a quarter each," I informed them.

Ellie put down her binoculars and looked me over. "Isn't the bow tie and hat you're wearing from our dress-up box?"

The kid paid his quarter and went into the tent.

"It sure is our stuff," Justin said, "and I want it back right now, or I'm going to go tell Mom."

"Okay, okay," I said, deciding it would be worth two more free seats to get the twins off my back. Besides, my customers were beginning to get restless. The noise level was getting pretty high in the tent. I didn't have time for a family fight. "Go on in, but sit by the door and be quiet. Then no more shows. You understand?"

Justin and Ellie nodded, then lifted their binoculars to their eyes and walked into the tent.

I followed them to the doorway and did a quick count. Eight paying customers. That was—I pulled out Mom's pocket calculator—$2.00. It's a start, I said to myself, and was just about to walk up front and begin the show when I turned and saw Bobbie Jo with what looked like a four-year-old girl by her side.

"This is my cousin Amy from Charleston, South Carolina," Bobbie Jo said, putting her hand on the girl's shoulder. "We've come to see the show."

I grabbed her two quarters and pocketed them. Bobbie Jo rolled her eyes, but I ignored her. Ten paying customers at a quarter each. That was . . . ten times twenty-five . . . $2.50! So now I only needed—Mom's calculator again—$22.64 more. Things were looking good!

And stayed looking that way all through my very first tarantula show. Sure, I was pretty nervous at the beginning. My voice caught: "And n-now!" Then came out too loud: "WHAT YOU ALL HAVE BEEN WAITING FOR!"

Justin and Ellie clapped their hands and yelled, "Yay, Ryan! Yay!"

I started to shush them—noisy brats!—but then lots of kids started clapping, too. I grinned and relaxed, even with Telly and Aaron right up front and Bobbie Jo watching closely from the side. If anyone went into the tent thinking I was just a short little sixth-grader acting like a kid, or some kind of a fool, they were in for a surprise. I put on a show. I picked Fang up, making a big deal out of how dangerous this was. "Don't try it at home," I said, acting like an expert.

Aaron jumped back when Fang started crawling up my arm. Telly laughed and poked him in the ribs, then winked at me.

Next, I fed Fang a cricket. He went for it just as fast as he had that time in front of Gordon. There was a big gasp from the audience.

"Yay! Yay!" Justin and Ellie yelled from the back. "Yay, Ryan!" The crowd started yelling it, too— except, I noticed, for Bobbie Jo.

But that didn't matter. I took off my hat and

bowed as everyone hollered and clapped, then bowed some more when they wouldn't stop. I was making money. I was a star. Just the kind of star that would be cool on the first day of junior high.

Cool. Cool. Totally cool.

CHAPTER 12

We Want Our Money Back!

I decided to celebrate the first show's success with a little snack—my favorite, a peanut butter and banana sandwich. I was standing at the kitchen counter, right in the middle of a big bite, when Mom walked in and said, "Have you thought about those signs you put up?"

"Jigra mngfnog," I said.

Mom frowned. "Don't talk with your mouth full, Ryan."

I swallowed my bite in a big gulp. "But you asked me a question."

She nodded. "Aren't you exaggerating a bit with your advertising? Granted, it's working. There *are* lots of kids out on the front lawn, but—"

"There are?" I said, and ran to the front window. At least a dozen kids were by the tent. "All right!" I yelled. "Customers!"

Actually it was more like "Awgrifgt! Cusmrrs!"

"Don't talk with your mouth full!" Mom said from the kitchen.

But I was already halfway out the front door.

To my surprise, a lot of the kids that had come to the first show were back for a rerun. Telly showed up alone, though. "Aaron has to practice his tuba," he said, then laughed. "No way. His mom makes him practice every day at five o'clock, not now. He's just afraid of that spider. Not me, though. I think it's cool."

I grinned from ear to ear. Telly—a seventh-grader who was a great basketball player—thought Fang was cool.

Several other of the kids were also return customers, but not all of them were returning *paying* customers.

Gordon came back. "I've got an idea," he said, "you're going to love."

I wasn't so sure about that.

"Put up fliers on telephone poles and on the bulletin board at the Stop and Go Mini-Mart. You can reel in huge crowds that way, and really cash in. I could be your marketing director!"

"Uh . . . I'll think about it," I said, pretty sure that I wouldn't. I didn't know what a marketing director was, but I was almost positive I didn't need one. Couldn't Gordon see all the business I had here? Things were booming without his help. He had his Slam Dunk Sky Jumpers. Now I needed to concentrate on getting mine.

Still, I let Gordon into the second show for free. Even if he kept grumbling, he deserved that much, I guessed.

The twins didn't, though. "No way, you guys," I said when they showed up again.

"But we just thought—"

"No quarter, no show," I said, and they could see that I really meant it. They started to turn away when another voice came from down the sidewalk.

"I'll pay for them to get in."

It was Bobbie Jo, walking toward me with her cousin Amy from Charleston. She reached into her pocket and pulled out a dollar bill. "This is for four people."

I took the dollar. Eleven paying customers this time. I whipped out Mom's calculator again. Eleven times twenty-five cents . . . $2.75! Now I needed only . . . $19.89 more for my Slam Dunk Sky Jumpers!

The second performance went even better than

the first, until feeding time. "And now!" I said. "Witness death right before your very eyes!"

I reached into the cricket jar and nabbed a victim. Slowly, I held it up for the crowd to see, then pulled back the cover of Fang's terrarium. "Watch closely. Tarantulas are very quick. They can pounce on their prey with the speed of light."

Everyone in the tent held their breath for one long moment as I dangled the cricket over Fang. Someone in the back whimpered, and I couldn't help smiling. "You are about to witness *death!*" I said. "Lights! Camera!" I dropped the cricket. "Action!"

Nope. As we all watched, holding our breaths, waiting like spectators at a car wreck, absolutely nothing happened. Fang just sat there, big and hairy. No pounce. No screams of horrified delight from the audience. Nothing. Absolutely nothing.

"Uh . . . he's just eyeballing his prey," I offered, willing Fang with all my might to get on with the show.

But he didn't. I reached in and gave the cricket a little nudge with my finger. Maybe if it moved a little closer, Fang would reach out and grab it.

But Fang didn't so much as move even one of his eight hairy legs.

"Come on," I heard someone say.

"Yeah," another voice chimed in.

I looked up and forced a smile. "Don't worry," I told the packed tent—eleven *paying* customers. "He'll eat."

But he didn't. Not even after I nudged the cricket again, and it jumped so close to Fang their noses almost touched. Then the cricket jumped again, this time on its own, and actually landed on Fang's back for a second before hopping off.

"We paid to see Fang the Killer," someone in the crowd said.

"That's right!" came another voice.

Panic crept up my spine. I grabbed the cricket and shoved it in front of Fang.

Again, nothing.

"I want my money back," a girl in the second row said, holding out her hand toward me.

"Me, too," a little boy beside her demanded.

I faced the crowd. "No. He'll eat. He's just . . . uh . . ." My mind was racing. I had to come up with something fast. In desperation, I looked around for anything to save the show. "Uh . . ."

Then I saw a piece of cardboard on the tent floor, left over from the sign making. I grabbed it and held it up. "Fang just needs some of his favorite exercise first!" I blurted out. "You know, to work up an appetite!"

I quickly lifted Fang out of his terrarium and held

him up for everyone to see. With my other hand, I rested one end of the cardboard on the table, and held the other up in the air. In my best ringmaster voice, I announced, "Fang happens to be the only spider in the world that likes to go down a slide. Right before I caught him, I saw him sliding down a steep bank deep in the heart of the Arizona wilderness, like a kid at the playground."

"Oooh!" said Amy from Charleston, eyes wide. "I like slides."

I smiled at her. But Bobbie Jo said, "I've never heard of *any* spider that goes down a slide."

This I did not need.

"*Oh yeah?*" I said, and started to push Fang down the cardboard just to show her how dumb people like her can be.

But before I could, Bobbie Jo jumped up and said, "You're going to hurt that poor thing!"

I glared at her. "I am not! You don't know anything about tarantulas! You're from Mississippi!"

Bobbie Jo stopped, and for a second I thought I'd shut her up. But then her green eyes seemed to turn as gray as steel. "I ran to the library after your last show," she said, drawing her words out like they were knives. "And I found *this*."

Bobbie Jo pulled a small book from her back pocket. "It's called *A Kid's Guide to Tarantulas*. See?"

She held it up so everyone would be sure she was telling the truth. There was the title, just like she'd said. "Nowhere in this book," she continued, "does it say that tarantulas like to go down slides. *Nowhere.*"

"Well . . . uh . . . ," I stuttered, "Fang is different, see. I told you that he is the only one in the world that—"

"*Nowhere* in this book," Bobbie Jo cut in, "does it say that tarantulas are deadly poisonous like you've been advertising, either. Their bite would hardly hurt a human, and they aren't likely to bite, anyway. And Fang couldn't be the largest one in captivity like the sign says. Sonoran tarantulas are not nearly as big as the ones that live in Brazil." She opened up *A Kid's Guide to Tarantulas* and quickly flipped the pages until she found what she wanted. "Right here on page eighteen it says, 'The largest tarantulas live in South America. The *Lasiodora* is found in Brazil and has a leg span of up to ten inches!' " She looked over at me. "That's *twice* as big as Fang!"

The crowd ooohed and ahhhed as they imagined a spider that big.

I shuffled around for a moment. "Uh . . . I knew that," I said, which was partly true. I hadn't known that the spider from Brazil was called *Lasiodora.* I'd

studied Arizona tarantulas, but most of what I knew
was from watching Fang and talking to people about
him.

Still, I didn't want to admit that in front of Bobbie Jo and everybody else. They were all staring,
waiting to hear my comeback. "What I meant on the
sign was that Fang is the largest *North American* tarantula in captivity," I said. "And he *is* deadly poisonous to a cricket."

There! That would put an end to that. Not bad
on such short notice.

But Bobbie Jo snorted and said, "You've been
telling some big ones, Ryan. Admit it."

I put on my best angry look and stared at Bobbie
Jo. (Dad says that the best defense is a good offense.)
"Well," I said, making my voice gruff.

"Well, *what*?" Bobbie Jo shot back, her eyes drill-
ing into me. "We get our money back?"

A chorus of voices rang out. "Yeah! We want our
money back!"

I scooped Fang up and quickly returned him to
his terrarium. The thought of running for it crossed
my mind. Then the thought of all those kids chasing
me down Sycamore Street crossed my mind, too.

"We want our money back!" a kid began to chant.
"We want our money back!" Another kid joined in,
then more picked up the chorus. "We want our
money back! We want our money back!"

Bobbie Jo continued to stare at me, and then I saw a flicker of something in her eyes. She thought this was funny! She actually enjoyed watching me squirm!

"We want our money back!" the crowd yelled. "We want our money back!"

I had absolutely no idea what to do.

CHAPTER 13

The Human Basketball

It's amazing what some people will do in a panic—stupid, crazy things that they wouldn't even consider on a normal afternoon. But that Sunday P.M. wasn't normal, and the idea I suddenly got wasn't normal, either. It just popped into my head.

"And now for the second act of this really great show!" I yelled above all the noise. "Follow me to the driveway, where for the first time in history you will witness a human basketball slam-dunk itself for two points!"

Telly's eyes went wide. "Do *what?*"

"Right this way! See the human basketball!" I

screeched before anybody could ask for a refund again. I bolted out of the tent and around the house, with everybody following me. I ran into the garage and got Dad's extension ladder. Quickly, I leaned it up against the backboard and climbed out of even Telly's tall reach.

Not that kids were grabbing for me. I just wanted to be sure that they didn't. All the money for two shows was in my pants pocket. I climbed up and over the backboard and perched like a red-tailed hawk on the rim of the basketball hoop.

"Right before your very eyes!" I shouted.

"Don't jump, Ryan!" Ellie called up, her voice trembling. "You could get hurt!"

Justin looked at her, then took off for the back door of the house yelling. "Mom! Mom! Ryan is acting crazy!"

Standing on the rim, the soles of my shoes ten feet off the ground, I had to admit that this did seem a little crazy and that a person could indeed get hurt pretending to be a basketball.

But I gulped back my fear and announced, "Ryan O'Keefe for two!"

Mom swung open the back door. "What in the world?" she said, then, "Ryan, NO!"

It was a good idea—that NO!—but too late. I'd already jumped.

*   *   *

My feet made it through. My legs made it through. My body made it through. But my elbows didn't. I must have had them sticking out like I do when I'm eating a hamburger, because they both got tangled in the net and I was left dangling like a fish on a line.

"Cool, Ryan," Telly said, looking up at me.

I looked down from where I hung—my head just under the rim, my feet swinging back and forth five feet off the ground—and tried to smile. "I think I was fouled."

Telly laughed. "Good one! Definitely a good one!"

Bobbie Jo stepped up beside Telly. "I've seen a lot of really dumb things in my life," she said, shaking her head in disgust, "but this has got to be the dumbest. You must have been at the end of the line when they handed out brains, Ryan."

I hate to admit it, but considering the position I was in, I couldn't argue the point.

Stupid or no, though, no one was yelling for their money back, and I wasn't hurt. Shaken up a bit, maybe. Tangled and dangling, maybe. But not much more than a scratch, I could tell.

Mom got me down, with some help from Telly. "What has gotten into you, Ryan?" she asked once she was sure I didn't need to go to the emergency room.

I shrugged. "I don't know."

"It's peer pressure," she mumbled, ushering me into the house. "I've been warned about junior high behavior, but what were you *thinking?*"

Mom decided that I wasn't thinking at all and sent me to my pink bedroom to do a little of it.

But first I brought in Fang from where I'd left him in the tent so I wouldn't worry about him out there all alone. Then I could really think.

Not about why I'd jumped through the net, though. That was clear enough—for the money! What I needed to think about was what to do next. This time I'd been lucky with the human basketball trick. But if Fang stopped cooperating for good, my show was a goner. And so were my pair of Slam Dunk Sky Jumpers. It was obvious that he wasn't going to eat every time *I* wanted him to, just when *he* wanted to. Which could be only two or three times a week. Which wouldn't do at all if I was going to make money fast. And after everything Miss-Know-It-All Bobbie Jo had said, waving *A Kid's Guide to Tarantulas* around, I couldn't keep using the same signs. So then how was I going to keep the shows going?

As I was considering all of this, Fang walked over

to the corner of his terrarium. He put one leg on the glass, then two, then all but one of his eight legs, and reached for the top.

I leaned closer. "Hey, old buddy," I whispered, "you're okay, aren't you? You'll perform for Ryan, right?"

Fang moved back from the corner toward the center of the terrarium, as if it were the center ring of the big-top and he was ready to perform again.

"Good boy!" I said, and reached into the terrarium to stroke my spider the way you would a dog. He reared up and tried to bite me.

I jerked my hand back so fast, I hit myself in the face.

"Whoa!" I leaned close to the glass. Fang was back down on all eight legs as if nothing had happened. "What was *that* all about?" I said. "I've picked you up bunches of times and you've never done that before."

I slowly reached back into the terrarium, this time with my hand in front of Fang. He walked up onto my fingers, then back onto the sand.

"Hmmm, what's the deal here?" I reached in again, coming straight down toward Fang's back.

He reared up and batted at my fingers with his front legs. I pulled my hand back, shaking my head. Why was he doing that?

Then I remembered. A tarantula's worst enemy

out in the desert is the tarantula wasp. It paralyzes poor little spiders like Fang with its sting and then buries them alive after laying its eggs on their body. Yuck! When the eggs hatch, the wasp larvae eat the fresh body. Aiyeee! Talk about terrible. Tarantula wasps attack from above. No wonder Fang was ready to bite my finger!

I did it again. And Fang reared up again, looking like a great monster fighting off the enemy.

"Cool," I said. And it was. As cool as watching him eat a cricket. Maybe even cooler!

I sat back down on my bed. I could already see the new signs announcing the incredible attraction: ALL NEW SHOW! SEE THE FIGHTING TARANTULA! Sure! All I had to do was put my finger over his back and Fang would rear up every time, even if he wasn't hungry. It would work. Who needed Gordon to come up with good ideas? I was as good a businessman as he was. I could make all the money I needed, no matter what Bobbie Jo said.

I jumped up and did a little dance in the middle of my bedroom floor. Yes! Yes! The show would go on!

CHAPTER 14

Yahoo!

I promised Mom that I would never be a basket-ball again.

She said, "I'm relieved to hear that."

Then I told her about the new signs. "He really will fight," I assured her. "You want to see?"

"No thank you," Mom said. "Remember, Fang is your pet, not a boxing glove."

I said, "I know. Don't worry."

Mom looked at me for a long moment and said, "I'll try."

I went to bed early, thinking about Monday, the last day before school started, and all I had to do before then. That night, I dreamed that I was sitting on top of a huge pile of Slam Dunk Sky Jumpers, and they were *all* mine.

In the morning, I put up the new signs—four of them—in front of the house. I also made ten fliers and posted them around the neighborhood and down at the Stop and Go Mini-Mart like Gordon had suggested.

And it worked. The tent was packed for the first three shows. Nobody mentioned the day before. I guess they figured they'd get their money's worth, one way or the other, even if it was watching me jump through the hoop.

Gordon showed up again, wanting a piece of the action. But this time I just told him no. Four-Star Sports closed at six o'clock. School started tomorrow. I needed every quarter I could get my hands on. Let me get my pair of Slam Dunk Sky Jumpers, then maybe we could talk about some kind of a partnership. But no free admission now. No way.

Gordon went stomping off, yelling, "If it wasn't for me, you'd be sitting on the front porch feeling sorry for yourself!" He shook his fist. "You can't get away with this, O'Keefe! Just you wait! I'll . . . I'll do *something!*"

I wanted to go after Gordon, but just then Telly came back, with Aaron this time. Aaron had bet Telly that he really wasn't a chicken. He'd prove it

by sitting in the front row, right next to Fang's terrarium, and not even flinch when I took Fang out.

The twins showed up again, too, but this time
didn't want to get into the show. Instead, they
wanted me to go with them to the doctor's office to
get their school shots. "Could you hold our hands
when he sticks us with the needle, Ryan?"

I said, "Nope."

Ellie looked around at the tent and sign and all the
kids. "You never help us anymore, Ryan," she said.
"Or play with us, either."

Justin nodded. "Or read *The Cat in the Hat*. Or let
us ride on your back. Or give us good-night hugs
and kisses. Why don't you like us anymore?"

A kid came up wanting to buy a ticket. "I don't
have time for this," I said to the twins, shooing them
away. "Can't you see that I'm busy? I'm making
money here."

And by the end of the day, I had indeed. Things
went perfectly.

Well, nothing is completely perfect. Telly kept
poking Aaron in the ribs during the first show and
saying, "You're afraid of Fang, aren't you?"

When Aaron started ignoring him, Telly put his
hand on Aaron's shoulder and yelled, "Tarantula!"
Aaron jumped up, and I thought he was going to
make his own door in the tent on the way out. Instead of running, though, he got mad and pushed

Telly over. From the look on Telly's face, I was sure there was going to be a fight right there in the middle of my show. But Telly just laughed like it was all a big joke. He acted as if he wasn't angry. But I heard him say under his breath, "I'll get Aaron back for that."

Like I said, nothing is *completely* perfect. But other than the kid named Billy who came to the third show and kept pretending he was picking buggers out of his nose and flicking them on the tent ceiling, the rest of the day went great.

Fang reared up and acted like he was fighting every time I put my finger over his back. He even decided he was hungry in the fourth show. It was great. He pounced on a cricket I had put in the corner of his terrarium, just as I was saying, "Despite all that has been written about tarantulas in books, many things are still unknown and unexpected." Pounce! Gotcha! You should have seen everyone jump.

By the fourth show, kids were beginning to line up outside the tent for the next performance. As soon as I was done dazzling one group, I rushed them out and flung back the tent door for the next group to come in. By four o'clock I had done seven packed shows. I was exhausted but also rich. I sat down on the front porch and counted my money. I knew I had done well, but not that well. I counted

once, then twice, then even a third time. I'd made it!
I had enough to buy my very own pair of Slam
Dunk Sky Jumpers at the regular price!

"YAHOO!" I yelled so loud, Mom and Dad came
running out onto the front porch to see if something
was wrong.

I begged them to let me go get the shoes right
away. "Pleeease! I've got the money! The store
closes at six!"

"Sure," Dad said so quickly that I instantly for-
gave him for moving us to Kentucky. "You deserve
that. You've worked hard for your money."

Mom shook her head and let out a big sigh. Then
she said, "If that's how you really want to spend
what you've earned, then go ahead. Just don't get
into such a hurry you forget to be careful, okay?"

"Okay!" I said, already halfway off the porch,
headed toward the garage. I jumped on my bike and
raced down Sycamore Street hill so fast, the wind
was screaming in my ears. I flew around the curve at
the bottom, scattering a bunch of ducks waddling
toward the creek. It felt like I was going at least a
hundred miles an hour.

"YAHOO!" I shouted for the whole world to
hear. A few more minutes and a pair of Slam Dunk
Sky Jumpers would be MINE, MINE, ALL
MINE!

CHAPTER 15

Genuine Marvels

After all the trouble I'd had saving the money to buy my Slam Dunk Sky Jumpers, I thought it would be pretty complicated actually buying a pair.

It wasn't, though. Mrs. Marcosa said, "Why, yes, we got in the new shipment right after lunch, and I have your size." She went into a storeroom and brought out a box. She pulled out the size-seven Slam Dunk Sky Jumpers, slipped them on my feet, and they fit.

I said I wanted to wear them home, of course. Mrs. Marcosa put my old shoes in a bag that I could sling over my bicycle handlebars. And before I knew it, I was at the cash register giving her nearly every penny I had in the world. Just like that! Money may be hard to come by, but it sure goes fast.

Riding my bike back up the Sycamore Street hill, I quickly forgot about the money, though. Despite the hot, humid afternoon, having a pair of Slam Dunk Sky Jumpers on my feet made me feel cool. And I was positive they made me stronger, too. The hill seemed less steep, the pedaling almost easy. In no time at all I was at the top.

I rode around the neighborhood, waving to everybody I saw: Aaron, who said he was headed home to practice his tuba; Telly, who was mowing his lawn. Circling back around to the top of the hill, I saw that Bobbie Jo was sweeping her front walk.

"Hi, y'all!" I called out to her, trying on a southern accent for size. It felt good. As a matter of fact, *everything* felt good. The sky was blue, the air full of flowery smells, and all the trees and grass a beautiful green. I pointed down. "Nice shoes, huh?"

Bobbie Jo leaned on her broom handle and looked at my Slam Dunk Sky Jumpers. "Genuine marvels," she said, but I could tell she didn't mean it.

I didn't care, though. What did she know? She was from Mississippi. She'd never make it here in good ol' Kentucky. Not like me, anyway. Not only was I cool; I was *really* cool. Look out, junior high school, here I come!

Back at home, I dropped my bike on the front

lawn. I took the old shoes out of the shopping bag. "Out with the old!" I said, and tossed them in the air. "Now in with the new!" I shouted, and ran straight to the basketball hoop.

Just as I thought it would, my first shot swished. Then my second. I was hot! I dribbled around the driveway, faked and drove for the basket. A hook over my head . . . zzzzzip again!

I could see it all. First I'd make the junior high team, then high school and the state tournament, just like Dad. Then on to the University of Kentucky, then the pros. Sure, I could do it!

I backed up and faced the basket again, imagining it was the NBA championship game. Five seconds remained on the clock. The crowd was on its feet, roaring as I brought the ball down the court. I drove for the basket, weaving, dribbling between my legs, then leaping into the air. A fake pass. I turned in midair. Around my back and over my head, higher than Hoop Richardson on the TV ad. Higher and higher still! SLAM DUNK, just like my shoes!

Really, I just laid it up. But it was a good shot, banked off the backboard as sweet as you please. I ran around and around under the basket with my arms raised. Ryan O'Keefe, NBA All-Star!

"Hi, Ryan."

I stopped. It was Justin. He and Ellie were standing beside the garage looking at me. He held up a small plastic toy spaceship. "I got this at the doctor's office," he said. "The nurse gave it to me because I was brave and only cried a little bit."

"A lot," Ellie said. "He cried a lot."

Justin ducked his head, but then raised it again and said, "Maybe we can make this little spaceship come to life and carry us to the moon to meet Quando. What do you think, Ryan?"

"Hmmmm," I said. "I think I'd stick with the refrigerator box rocket you've been building. Mount it on your bikes. That way you could get up more speed for takeoff."

"Good idea!" Ellie said.

Justin nodded. "Thanks, Ryan. You're acting like you again."

They both ran over and gave me a hug. Ellie said, "We like it when you're you!"

I pointed down. "See?" I said. "See my new shoes? They're Slam Dunk Sky Jumpers!"

Justin leaned close. "Wow! They look like the best shoes ever made!"

Ellie squatted down and touched them with one finger. "They're nice, Ryan, really, *really* nice." Then they both ran off singing, "We're going to the moon! We're going to the moon!" as Mom called from the kitchen window, "I've got a favor to ask."

"Okay," I said. I took one more shot, which swished—of course—and then I went inside.

Mom was unpacking what looked like the last of the kitchen boxes. "Your father and I just realized that tonight is the anniversary of our first date," she said, putting the blue coffee cups in a row on the counter. "Fourteen years ago he asked me out for dinner."

It was hard to imagine—them going out on a date before I was even born. It was also hard to imagine them not knowing each other, then getting to know each other, falling in love and all that junk. It was hard to imagine, but I could tell by Mom's smile that it meant a lot to her.

"Cool," I said.

She smiled even bigger. "We'd like to take a break from all this unpacking and work on the house and celebrate over dinner, just the two of us. I know this is short notice, but could you look after Justin and Ellie while we're gone?" She went over to the refrigerator and took out a package of hot dogs. "I'll fix you something to eat," she said, holding them up. "Your favorite."

"Yum," I said, suddenly very hungry. "Sure, I'll baby-sit. No problem."

Mom gave me a hug. "Thank you! You're such a wonderful son!"

I grinned, amazed at how much difference a new pair of shoes—the *right* shoes—could make. I felt just as wonderful as Mom said.

Until about halfway through dinner. Justin and Ellie were going on and on about meeting Quando on the moon and how they were going to mount the spaceship box on their bicycles, just like I'd suggested. I was nodding when suddenly I remembered Fang. I'd been so excited about finally having enough money to buy my Slam Dunk Sky Jumpers, I'd clean forgotten about my good old spider. After all he'd done for me, I'd gone rushing off to Four-Star Sports and left him outside in the tent, all alone. "Oh no!" I said, jumping up from the table.

Justin and Ellie stopped short and looked at me. "We can't tie the spaceship box onto our bikes with shoestrings?" Ellie asked.

Justin put his hot dog down on his plate. "Then how would we do it, Ryan? We meet Quando on the moon *tonight*."

Without answering, I rushed past the twins, through the living room, and out the front door. "Fang?" I called toward the show tent. How could I have been so selfish? Without him, I would never have gotten my shoes. *"Fang?"*

I hurried down the front porch steps, across the yard, and into the tent. "Hey, ol' buddy, sorry I forgot about—"

But then I saw. Although Fang's terrarium was still on the card table, inside it there was no Fang.

CHAPTER 16

The Voice of a Thief

I ran over to the terrarium. "Fang?" I lifted the rock and scraped in the sand. "*Fang?*"

Fang was gone. I looked all around. "Fang! FANG!"

Nothing. He was nowhere in sight. Someone had stolen him. Someone had come into the tent and taken my wonderful spider when I was downtown buying my Slam Dunk Sky Jumpers. Or when I was shooting baskets around back. Or in the house eating dinner with the twins.

But *who?* Who would do such a lowdown thing to me? I slammed my fist down on the card table. Gordon! It had to be Gordon! He'd been jealous of all the money I'd been making from the very beginning. And he'd threatened to get even somehow. It had to be him. He was the thief! Gordon!

I whirled and almost ran smack into the twins, who were standing in the tent doorway.

Ellie said, "We decided to tie the box onto our bicycles with yarn from Mom's knitting basket instead of shoestrings."

Justin's eyes were wide with excitement. "Then we're going to take off from the big hill! What do you think of that?"

"Not now," I said. I was so angry at Gordon, I could hardly see straight.

"What's wrong, Ryan?" Ellie said.

"NOT NOW!" I yelled, then bulled my way past, pushing them out of the way. I had to hurry to catch Gordon the spider thief red-handed. And after I did, I was going to show him just how tough Arizona boys could be!

Although I was mad enough to go tearing right in the front of Gordon's house without knocking (the way he always did at our house), I was smart enough not to. Gordon had told me that he sometimes snuck out his bedroom window by climbing onto the back porch roof, then down the maple tree. I sprinted around the side of the house, then quickly but quietly climbed up the tree and eased myself over the gutter and onto the roof. I tiptoed across to Gordon's window, which was partway open. The light was on, and I could hear a voice inside. It was the voice of a thief—Gordon's voice.

I peered over the windowsill to see Gordon standing in front of a mirror. "Hi, my name is Gordon," he was saying. "What's yours?" He frowned. "No, not cool enough for junior high girls." He turned a bit to the side and put his hands in his pockets, then slouched and stuck his lower lip out a bit. "Hey, babe, what's happening?" he said, bobbing his head up and down like it was on a spring.

If I hadn't been so angry at Gordon, I would have burst out laughing right then. I had no idea that he practiced conversations in front of the mirror. How goofy!

Well, okay, so I practice what I'm going to say sometimes before I say it, too. And yeah, sure, I've stood in front of the mirror before, checking out how I looked. But I didn't look goofy like Gordon . . . did I?

"Yeah, cool," Gordon said, nodding at himself. He moved over to his closet and started rummaging around in a pile of clothes on the floor.

I quickly forgot about whether or not I might actually look goofy in front of the mirror as my anger came flooding back. I pulled myself up so I could see better. Gordon was facing away from me, but I was sure he was covering something up with a T-shirt and a pair of underwear. It looked like a large jar.

Fang! Gordon had swiped my spider and put him in a jar. The thief! The rotten, low-down thief!

I stood up and grabbed the screen, ready to push it up and throw myself into Gordon's room like I'd seen cops do on TV. But there was a low growl, and suddenly Colonel was in my face. Teeth bared, Gordon's dog hit the screen from inside, putting a big dent in it with his nose. I fell back in surprise and, with a wild scream—"Yeoooooooooooow!"—rolled off the porch roof.

CHAPTER 17

Get Him!

Crashing through limb after tree limb toward Gordon's backyard, I squeezed my eyes shut, not wanting to see myself hit the ground. When I finally landed, it was with a great thud, and I was sure that I'd probably broken something. How could I fall that far and not at least crack a few bones?

Still, I didn't hurt. The only thing I noticed different about my body was that my nose was full of the smell of flowers.

That was when it hit me. Funeral flowers! I'd gone and *killed* myself. Yikes! How awful!

But then I thought that if I really was dead, and this was my funeral, then everyone would be sitting around feeling sorry, talking about what a great kid

I'd been. "Poor Ryan," they'd all say. "He was one in a million . . . a billion . . . a *trillion!*"

I decided that I liked the idea that everybody would say wonderful things about me. Maybe being dead wasn't going to be so bad. I opened my eyes to see what it looked like, expecting lots of pretty lights, maybe an angel or two.

But what I saw instead of lights or angels was Colonel charging out of Gordon's back door, followed by Gordon, who was yelling something about a burglar trying to sneak into his bedroom window but who fell off the porch roof into the flowerbed.

Burglar? Ha! What a nitwit Gordon was! It had been *me* on the roof, and this was my funeral, because now I was dead.

Or was I? A quick glance and I could see all of me in one piece, not hurt, lying in the middle of a flowerbed as if it were siesta time. I was okay! It was a miracle! Hitting all those tree limbs on the way down had broken my fall. And I'd landed on soft earth instead of the brick patio just a foot away. I'd fallen off a porch roof and lived to tell about it! I was alive!

Although maybe not for long. Colonel was bearing down on me like an angry grizzly bear. Gordon was now pointing at me and yelling, "There he is! Get the burglar, Dad! Get him!" And Gordon's dad was running toward me with a baseball bat in his hand.

A baseball bat?

"It's me!" I yelled, jumping up and waving my arms. "It's Ryan!"

Colonel stopped short, his little doggy toenails scraping on the patio bricks like fingernails on a chalkboard. Gordon tripped over Colonel and went down like a sack of potatoes. Gordon's dad stumbled over both of them. As he lurched forward, the baseball bat flew out of his hand and went flying past me within an inch of my ear.

"DON'T KILL ME!" I screamed. "I ALMOST DIED ONCE ALREADY!"

I didn't like the look in Gordon's dad's eyes as he struggled to get up off the patio. I offered him a hand and tried to make myself smile. "Hi," I said. "I just came by to . . . uh . . ."

"*To what?*" Gordon said, glaring up at me. He was holding his left knee, which I could see was bleeding a little, and it was plain that he was angrier than his dad would ever be.

Which made me angry. In an instant, I forgot all about falling, funerals, miracles, and excuses, and came back to accusations. "I'm here to get my spider," I yelled at Gordon. "Because you stole it, *thief!*"

Gordon spent a split second looking completely dumbfounded, then jumped to his feet. "I didn't steal your stupid spider! Is this the way people in Arizona treat their friends? By accusing them of being crooks? I'm not a crook!" He got right up in my face. "*You're* the crook, Ryan, taking all my business advice and then not sharing any of the profits. You probably hid Fang somewhere so you could collect insurance, or get lots of publicity and then make even more money on your dumb little shows!"

"My shows aren't dumb!" I shot back. "And if you're not the thief, then what did I see you hiding in your closet? Huh? *Huh?*"

Gordon rolled his eyes. "That was my penny jar, air brain. I've got three thousand five hundred and seventy-three pennies in it. I've been collecting them since I was three years old." He put his hands on his hips and snarled, "So there!"

Gordon's dad, I noticed, had recovered enough from my falling out of the sky into his flowerbed to be listening carefully. "Wait a minute," he said to Gordon. "I thought I told you to deposit those pennies in your bank account so they could be earning interest."

Gordon shuffled his feet around, suddenly looking sheepish. "Well . . . ," he said, glancing at his dad, "I like to count them at night. It helps me get to sleep."

His father frowned. "Get to sleep? Knowing your money is earning interest while it sits safely in the bank should make you rest better, not running your fingers through a jar of coins!"

"But I like the feeling!" Gordon said.

"Having invested wisely is all the good feeling anyone needs," Gordon's father insisted.

And so it went, father and son arguing over the best way to use a jarful of pennies.

Which left me standing there—*alive*—and free to consider another question: If Gordon didn't steal Fang, then who did? Who? *Who?* In my mind, I went over it again and again until, just as suddenly as I had thought of Gordon, I knew the answer.

"Gotta go!" I said, and raced past Gordon and his dad before they had a chance to protest. Down their driveway I sprinted, then up Sycamore Street as fast as my Slam Dunk Sky Jumpers would carry me. Running, running, to catch a thief.

CHAPTER 18

Fangnapping

Despite how sure I was that it was Telly who had stolen Fang—so he could get Aaron back for pushing him over in the tent—the sight of Telly's big stone house on Mildred Street brought me to a quick stop. I stood on the sidewalk in front of it, panting like a poodle from my run, and couldn't help wondering how somebody like me, a short sixth-grader, was going to get my spider back from a very tall seventh-grader who might very well be the best basketball player in junior high.

Just then a side door opened and Telly stepped out. He turned down the driveway in my direction. I ducked behind a tree and watched as he walked toward Aaron's house. He was carrying a plastic tub like we used at home to hold leftovers.

Fang! Telly had Fang in there and was going to scare Aaron with him. I was right! He *was* the thief!

Staying close to the bushes, I followed Telly as he turned the corner. Even though Aaron lived several houses down, I could hear him practicing his tuba. *Oompah, oompah, blat, pfftb.* No wonder his parents made him play in the garage. The tuba sounded like a sick elephant.

Telly ducked low and began to walk slowly on tiptoes when he got to Aaron's driveway. I slipped behind a hedge and crept alongside. Through the open door of Aaron's garage, I could see a big blue car parked on one side. Aaron was sitting on the other side, near the back wall on a riding lawn mower. His eyes were closed in concentration as his cheeks puffed in and out like balloons. *Oompah, oompah, blat, pfftb.* Whew! A sick elephant with a megaphone.

Telly crept closer, until he was right at the garage door opening. He raised the plastic container up over his head. He was going to throw Fang on Aaron!

"NO!" I yelled.

Telly jumped straight into the air. The plastic tub went flying.

"FANG!" I screamed.

I plunged through the hedge, throwing myself under the container to catch it. I hit the concrete driveway and rolled onto my back. I looked up to see the plastic tub slowly turn over in midair. What dumped out of it was not Fang. What hit me right in the face was at least a gallon of ice-cold water.

Telly looked at me, lying there soaking wet on the concrete, then over at Aaron. Startled by the commotion, Aaron had toppled backward off the riding lawn mower and lay pinned to the garage floor with his head stuck in his tuba. Although muffled, you could hear him yelling, "Get this thing off of me!"

The corners of Telly's mouth began to twitch. He turned back to me. "I was going to dump all that water down Aaron's tuba," he said, a smile working its way quickly across his lips. "But it looks just as good all over you!" He began to laugh. "And I love where Aaron ended up. I couldn't have planned it better. A double joke! I actually pulled off a double! This is funny, *very* funny!"

Not as far as I was concerned. I got up off the driveway, glaring, and said, "Did you steal my spider?"

Telly let out an even bigger hoot of laughter. "Steal your spider? Man, you're a jokester, too!" He stopped laughing and cocked his head to one side. "Not a bad idea, though. Except I might get arrested and charged with Fangnapping." He started laughing again. "Get it? Fangnapping? Get it, O'Keefe?"

I got it, but I didn't want it. I was so mad, I was ready to scream. None of this would have happened if we hadn't moved to Kentucky. It was Dad and Mom's fault for getting new jobs, the twins' fault for bugging me all the time. It was Gordon's fault for having my shoes and Telly's for being tall and full of dumb jokes. And it was Bobbie Jo's fault for moving to Macinburg and acting like it was no big deal, like I was a wimp because I hated it here.

I could just imagine how Bobbie Jo would laugh when she heard that Fang was missing. She'd shake her head at how stupid I was and act like she knew everything there was to know about anything. She'd probably laugh even more than Telly, thinking the best joke of all was that someone had stolen Fang and I couldn't figure out who had done it, and—

But wait a minute! The truth hit me so hard I almost fell down. Why hadn't I seen this to begin with? It was Bobbie Jo! Of course! *She* took Fang!

Furious—at Bobbie Jo for being so low and at myself for not seeing it earlier—I stomped away from Aaron's house and headed straight toward the Websters'.

CHAPTER 19

Stop!

Bobbie Jo's cousin Amy from Charleston was out on the front lawn, dancing in a tutu, when I came racing up.

"Where's Bobbie Jo?" I demanded.

"Bobbie Jo!" she yelled at the house without breaking from her twirl. "That nut from Arizona is here!"

I couldn't believe the pipsqueak was talking about me like that. But before I could do anything about it, Bobbie Jo opened the front door.

"Give me back my tarantula!" I yelled at her.

Bobbie Jo's eyes went wide. A look of surprise crossed her face, but it only stayed for a second.

She shook her head in disbelief. "Just how long have you been practicing to be a blockhead? You'd better go back to Arizona and look for your brain."

"I wish I *could* go back to Arizona!" I shouted. "But I can't! Fang is all I've got left of the desert, and you stole him, and I want him *now!*"

Bobbie Jo laughed. "I don't have your spider."

"Yes, you do," I screeched, "and it's not funny!" I was so mad, I was spitting my words out.

She laughed again, and I felt like hitting her, even if she was a girl. But just as I was about to decide it didn't matter if she was a girl or not, she suddenly pointed toward Sycamore Street and yelled, "Look!"

I wasn't in the mood for anymore jokes. "Don't try to pull that one on me!" I shouted.

"Stop!" Bobbie Jo yelled, and jumped off her porch toward me.

I balled up my fists and prepared to slug it out with the Mississippi smart-mouth.

But Bobbie Jo ran right past me. "Stop!" she yelled again, jumping the curb and sprinting down the street. "Stop!"

I turned and called after her. "Hey, what . . . where are you going?"

Then I saw what Bobbie Jo was yelling at, and a

shiver ran up my spine. There were Justin and Ellie, on their bicycles with the spaceship box mounted over them. They were pedaling like crazy, picking up speed entirely too fast, heading straight down the Sycamore Street hill.

CHAPTER 20

Quando
the Spaceman

I ran after them, the soles of my Slam Dunk Sky Jumpers slapping the pavement faster and faster. I pumped my arms and pushed forward as hard as I'd ever pushed in my entire life.

But I couldn't catch up. Bobbie Jo stayed out front, and in front of her were Justin and Ellie. No matter how hard I tried, no matter how new and expensive my shoes were, I couldn't gain on them.

"Stop!" Bobbie Jo and I both yelled.

But the twins didn't. If they could hear us, they ignored us. Down the Sycamore Street hill they steered their spaceship, faster and faster with every second, until it started to swerve.

A car came around the curve at the bottom of the

123

hill and started up. Bobbie Jo waved her arms as she ran. "Car!" she shouted. "Look out for the car!"

"Yeah, look out!" I screamed.

The spaceship straightened out just in time and safely passed the car on the right. Then it picked up even more speed. I kept running after the twins, going so fast I almost pitched face first onto the asphalt.

But it was no use. "Look out!" I screamed again, watching helplessly as the spaceship missed the curve at the bottom of the hill. It bounced over the curb, shot across the freshly mown Kentucky blue-grass, and sailed off the creek bank into the air, acting for all the world as if it really were taking off for the moon.

Bobbie Jo was just clearing the curb at the bottom of the hill when I finally passed her. I flew through the air and landed in the grass, immediately tripping over the root of a tree. I fell forward and skidded on my chest to a stop at the edge of the creek bank.

Justin and Ellie's spaceship was on its side in the shallow water below me. They were nowhere to be seen, and there were no sounds from inside the box.

I jumped to my feet and leaped halfway down the creek bank. But it was wet and slippery, so I skidded the rest of the way, arms flailing, trying not to end up on my bottom.

Instead, I went forward, falling splat on my face. I staggered to my feet, covered from head to toe with slimy dark mud.

"*Justin?*" I yelled. "*Ellie?*" I stumbled through the creek water over to the spaceship. "Are you all right? Hey, you guys, *speak to me!*"

Nothing. I searched frantically for the spaceship door, finally found it, tore it open, expecting to see the broken, bloody bodies of my brother and sister.

Justin and Ellie were in one corner of the box, piled there like dirty laundry. They both looked up at me for a second, a strange mixture of fright and surprise on their faces. Then Ellie broke into a big grin.

"We made it!" she cried. "We made it to the moon!"

Justin pointed straight at me. "Yeah, look!" he said, his eyes shining like pie pans in the sun. "It's Quando the spaceman!"

CHAPTER 21

Pretty Cool

For a moment I stood there looking down at Justin and Ellie, and I almost started crying. Not sad crying, but glad, glad that they were okay.

Then Justin pulled a hot dog from his pocket. "We brought this for you, Quando," he said. "It's food from our dinner table on Earth." He held it out for me.

But the hot dog slipped from Justin's fingers, did a double flip, and landed on top of my mudcaked shoe. Slam Dunk Sky Jumpers à la hot dog. I started laughing at the sight of it, a wave of relief washing over me.

"That's not Quando!" Ellie said. "Not even a spaceman could laugh that much like Ryan!"

Justin reached up from the corner of the toppled spaceship. "Ryan! You came to the moon, too!"

I laughed even harder and pulled the twins from the box. "No, we're in Kentucky," I said. "We're home." Then, there in the middle of the creek, I gave them a big mud-covered hug.

"Well, that's a who'd-a-thought-it," Bobbie Jo said quietly. I turned to see her standing at the top of the creek bank, green eyes sparkling. She smiled, and I couldn't help smiling back.

Bobbie Jo and I helped the twins climb the slippery bank. I hauled their bicycles out of the muck, and their soggy spaceship, too.

By the time we reached the top of the hill, it was beginning to get dark. Back at the house, I took off my muddy Slam Dunk Sky Jumpers and left them on the front walk. I changed and washed up while Bobbie Jo helped Justin and Ellie get into pajamas and ready for bed.

When I went into the twins' bedroom, Justin said, "Will you read us a story, Ryan?"

"I know just the one," I said. It took me a minute to find it, but when I pulled *The Cat in the Hat* off the shelf, Ellie said, "Oh!"

The twins sat in my lap while I read to them. They insisted that Bobbie Jo sit close by, so she could see the pictures.

After the story, I tucked the twins in. Bobbie Jo

sang the fried ham song so softly, it sounded like a lullaby. I found myself singing along: "Fried ham, fried ham, cheese, and bologna . . ."

Ellie said, "You sing nice, Ryan."

Justin nodded. "Even better than that!"

I laughed and said, "Thanks." I gave them each a hug, and a kiss, too.

At the front door, I turned on the porch light for Bobbie Jo. She said good night and started down the steps. I followed, calling, "Hey, thanks for the help." She stopped and looked back. I fidgeted around for a second, then added, "I'm sorry about the things I said over at your house."

Bobbie Jo smiled and, before I knew what was happening, came back up the steps and gave me a kiss on the cheek. "See you tomorrow at school," she said, and was gone.

All the blood seemed to rush to my head. I felt dizzy and had to sit down on the porch steps. I squeezed my eyes shut, then popped them open and looked out into the night. It took a few seconds, but my vision finally cleared.

The first thing that came into focus were my Slam Dunk Sky Jumpers, lying where I had left them on the sidewalk. I could also see my old shoes, on the lawn where I'd thrown them earlier. If I hadn't known, though, I wouldn't have been able to tell which was which. One pair muddy, the other smudged with desert dirt, in the dim glow of the front porch light, each looked as good as the other. All that money and energy and trouble, and from where I sat, I couldn't see any difference.

Except there was something about the old pair—the left shoe of the old pair.

I stood up and stared. Hmmmm. Maybe the dim porch light and darkening night shadows were playing tricks on my eyes. I was really tired. It had been a long day.

But then I thought I saw something move inside the shoe. I walked down the porch steps. I crept out onto the grass and leaned closer . . . just as my tarantula crawled out onto the shoelaces.

"Fang!" I yelled, and swept him up on his old-shoe perch. "Is that really you?"

It really was.

Not long after I'd gotten Fang settled back in his terrarium and the lid put on tight (he'd pushed up one corner to escape, I figured out), Mom and Dad came home. When they asked what the twins and I had done while they were gone, I said, "Took a wild spaceship ride to the moon. But we landed in Kentucky."

They both laughed.

I said, "Ask Justin and Ellie."

But they just kept on laughing.

I shrugged and said, "I've been thinking that I should go with you to take Justin and Ellie to their kindergarten class tomorrow, before I go to junior high. I could tell them what it was like for me when I first started school, give them a few tips."

Mom looked at me for a moment, then nodded and said, "That's very nice of you, Ryan. Very mature."

Dad patted me on the shoulder. "He's growing up!"

I rolled my eyes but had to smile. Come to think of it, I did feel different than I had when the day started. Not a completely new person. Just a little more grown-up, maybe, like Dad said.

Which didn't mean that life was going to be one big happy-ever-after from then on. I still had schedules and new teachers' names to learn at junior high, and a locker combination to remember. And probably classes to run for on opposite ends of the building. And big seventh- and eighth-graders who would hog the ball during basketball games after lunch. And swirlies to avoid. And on top of all that, at least two more apologies to make: to Gordon and Telly, for accusing them of stealing Fang. It wasn't going to be easy.

But after everything that had happened with Justin and Ellie, all that stuff didn't seem as important as it had before. I figured I would probably be able to handle it, no matter what brand of shoes I put on in the morning.

After saying good night to Mom and Dad, I climbed into bed and turned off the light. Although Mom still hadn't started painting yet, the moonlight that filled the room made the walls look less pink. Through the window I could see the moon—beautiful, silvery, a Kentucky moon.

Quando's moon, too, I thought with a smile. Crazy twins. They really were . . . well, pretty cool.

"Good night, Justin," I whispered up toward their room. "Good night, Ellie." I slowly closed my eyes . . . just as my bedroom door flew open, slamming into the wall.

I shot straight up off the mattress with a scream—"Aygh!"—and landed on the floor.

Justin and Ellie ran in. "Ryan! Ryan!" they yelled. "Quando is coming back!"

They waved their stuffed animals in my face. "Sleepy Bear and Hippo are going to fly with him to *Jupiter!* We've got to get the spaceship ready! Get up, Ryan! Get up, NOW!"